Precious Gold, Precious Jade

Precious Gold, Precious Jade

SHARON E. HEISEL

Holiday House · New York

Library of Congress Cataloging-in-Publication Data
Heisel, Sharon E.
Precious gold, precious jade / by Sharon E. Heisel.—1st ed.
p.   cm.
Summary: A young woman befriends a Chinese family despite
the racism and fear that overwhelm the residents of her small western
mining town at the end of the gold rush.
ISBN 0-8234-1432-9
[1. Prejudices—Fiction.   2. Gold mines and mining—Fiction.
3. Chinese—United States.   4. Racism—Fiction.
5. Murder—Fiction.]   I. Title.
PZ7.H3688 Pr   2000
[Fic]—dc21
                                                      98-027876

*This book is
dedicated
to my sister,
Diane Blackwell,
who is more precious
than both gold
and jade.*

Chapter 1

THERE'S SOMETHING ABOUT the first day of any-thing that makes a person cautious. I snuggled extra close to my little sister, Evangeline, protected by her warmth and Mama's quilts. Breakfast sounds and laughter filled our cabin, and I stole an extra moment, enjoying the certain-sure knowledge that I was exactly where I belonged.

I felt cautious but excited, too. The new school session was to start that day. Liza would be there, and this year we would be sitting in the next-to-last row. I didn't get to see her much during the summer, for she lived on the far side of Bounty.

Of course, we did meet at church every Sunday, but that wasn't entirely satisfying. We were expected to behave perfectly respectful.

I swung out of bed and fairly jumped into my clothes. Once in the kitchen, I danced beside the stove to warm myself. "Morning, Mama. Morning, Pa."

I'm not widely known for being talkative, first thing. I knew my brother, Tom, didn't expect a separate greeting from me so soon after waking.

"Good morning, Angelena." Mama put a plate of fresh griddle cakes on the table and beckoned me over.

Evangeline came in looking sleepy as a cat in cold weather. She plunked herself down beside Tom, and I sat across from him. Mama stooped to pick up little Reuben, stroked his hair back from his face, and bounced him gently.

Tom poured syrup over his griddle cakes. He had changed over the summer. He was taller and more muscled, but most of all more private. His dark eyes were lively, like Pa's, and he grinned at me around a mouthful of food.

"You'll have to look out for rattlesnakes and bullies on your own now."

Tom teased dreadfully, but he always kept an eye out for me. He was plenty big and strong enough to handle any bully.

He could handle a pick or shovel, too, and that was a useful talent in the diggin's. He had been smiles-all-over when the autumn rains finally came to gold country.

Each fall, miners and part-time farmers, like Pa, waited anxiouslike for the rains. A good year brought plenty of water to carry gold out of streambed gravels. Every day of digging and dredging meant more gold at cleanup time, and that meant more money to keep our farm growing.

Tom drew in a long swig of coffee and smacked his lips noisily. "You go and get smart. I'll help Pa get rich."

"Not much danger of me getting rich," Pa said, pushing back from the table. "Used to be a man could rightly prosper in the gold fields, but cleanup hasn't yielded much the past few years. Still, there's no sin in hoping and less sin in trying."

Pa never gave up the hope of a big strike, but he always took care of farm and family first. Tom was more inclined to depend on luck, but neither of them shirked hard work.

With harvest nearly finished and the rains rightly started, the town council had decided it was time to begin a new school term. Tom preferred to work the diggin's and Pa was glad for his help. After some discussion it was concluded that Evangeline and I should attend school.

I was fourteen, born next after Tom. No one would have noticed if I stayed home to help Mama, but she especially wanted me to get educated. She had talked with gentle words, but her tone had been rock solid.

"Angelena, you have a good mind. You must learn to use it well."

I allowed that I had a liking for books, at least more than Tom did. It was agreed that I should attend school at least one more year. With Tom at the diggin's,

3

Evangeline would be my responsibility, for she was only in the second grade.

I was mostly glad for my sister's company, but relieved that little Reuben was too young for school. It felt like liberation to leave him home.

He watched from Mama's arms as Evangeline and I set off for the village, each of us carrying our lunch and a book for the school. I waved with my free hand, feeling the rich joy of home side by side with the excitement of beginning.

Night rains had plumped the thick layer of pine needles on the forest floor. They muffled our footsteps and sprang up again after we went by, as if they were sending us along. I heard a woodpecker knocking somewhere out of sight, and the twitter of extra-tiny bush birds. Evangeline held my hand as we passed the Gustafsons' place, walking wide around the spot where a rattler bit their dog last summer.

"Oh look, Angelena. It's bound to be a good luck sign." She dropped my hand and pointed to part of a rainbow shimmering in the mist above their pond.

I was inclined to agree.

Chapter
2
❖

THE PLANK BRIDGE over Bunkum Creek thumped like a great drum as we crossed into town. On our left was the main part of Bounty, and past that was the section we called China Shacks. Beyond China Shacks, the road wound south beside the creek down toward the Rogue River. Mining claims dotted the banks of Bunkum Creek all the way to the Rogue.

Evangeline skipped ahead as we turned up Main Street. I hurried to catch up, past the tight-shuttered bank and the cinnamon-rich smells coming out of Wilson's Bakery. I minded Mama and made sure Evangeline didn't look into the gambling saloon, but I did steal a peek for myself. It wasn't much of a thrill, though, since all the miners were occupied at their diggin's. The place got busy after dark, I guess, but I can't say from my own experience. It's only what I've heard.

A huge oak marked our school yard at the edge of the village. There wasn't anything beyond but

Cemetery Hill. The schoolhouse looked like an ordinary cabin from the outside, but the minute we stepped over the high sill we couldn't pretend it was anything but a school.

Five rows of wood benches stood on the left, matched by another five on the right. The center aisle was broad enough to keep kids on either side from pestering each other, and plenty wide for Miss Jensen to get to the back of the room in a hurry, if she saw any mischief. With three on each bench, the school could hold thirty students. The town council must have expected Bounty to grow.

WELCOME filled the big chalkboard at the front of the room. Miss Jensen stood beside her high-backed chair, wearing a starched dress, with her hair looking a mite starchy, too. She had a tight grip on her shiny brass bell, ready to corral us for lessons. Her soft eyes and firm chin echoed the "welcome" and declared "no nonsense" at the same time.

The way it works at our school, Miss Jensen brings her own books and the families send books along, too, if they have any. All those books get put in one great heap and Miss Jensen assigns them to us. Sometimes we each get our own; other times we have to share.

Last year I had shared *The Young Ladies' Guide to Our Flower Friends* with Liza. I do love counting the seasons by the flowers, but this book had what Pa calls "More stuffin' than learnin'." We read about the "blossoms-in-waiting" and "murmurous bees" until I feared I would giggle out loud.

There was already a sizable stack of books on the table. Evangeline and I were mouse-quiet as we added ours, but I glimpsed an unfamiliar book about flowers.

"Thank you, girls."

"Yes, ma'am." I couldn't help asking, "Did you bring some new books back from your trip to San Francisco?"

"Yes, I did. There are actual booksellers there, and we needed some more challenging work for some of our better students."

"She must mean you and Tony," Evangeline looked at me kind of smuglike. She did like to tease about Tony.

"And others. We can never tell what new students may show up. All sorts of people seek education."

"Is it true they have buildings there tall as trees?" Evangeline sounded as if she thought that must be a fairy tale.

"Buildings *taller* than trees, and sailing ships that bring people from just about everywhere." Miss Jensen's eyes went dreamy; then she gave us her matter-of-fact look. "It's a wonderful big city to visit, but I enjoy coming home, too."

She looked around the school world she had created for us with some satisfaction. To me, the classroom looked pretty much the same as when classes let out last spring, only maybe it was a little neater. At least it seemed neater until the four youngest Gustafson kids made a rackety entrance and caused a flurry hanging up their coats.

Gustafsons can't seem to help causing a flurry. Tony laughed out loud. Mae bustled and fussed over her younger brother, George. Sarah, the youngest, stood shyly in the doorway until she spotted Evangeline. Evangeline saw Sarah at the same moment and hastened to take part in the commotion. Outside on the porch, the Gustafsons' new dog barked with considerable enthusiasm. The room felt brimful.

It was just as I remembered and just what I had hoped for. In our little town, school was like an extension of home, only a bit more interesting sometimes. I was especially glad to see Tony there. He was old enough for his family to decide he was needed at home, but I knew he valued school, for he had a mighty curiosity. Nothing much had changed, and my cautious feelings faded entirely.

Coat pegs on the back wall were already half-full and a pile of lunch buckets cluttered the shelf below. I didn't have to stretch at all to reach a top peg, but I hung my sweater in the middle row. The tall boys liked the highest pegs.

Evangeline hung hers next to Sarah's and they scurried off to find their seats. I had already spotted mine.

Liza McCutcheon sat tall on a bench in the next-to-last row. She wore a starched cotton dress that I recognized from seeing it on Belle, her older sister. I felt cheerful about finding Liza already there, especially when she grinned and patted the bench. I grinned back and settled beside her.

Muffled giggles drifted back from Evangeline and her friends at the front of the room. The littlest ones were always closest to the teacher and I was glad to have worked my way back so far. Liza and I started to catch up on our news.

"Isn't Tom coming?" Her nose wrinkled and her head jutted forward as she peered toward the door. She squished her eyes into little slits, as if she were looking into bright sunlight.

Liza has golden hair with just enough red to make it seem to glow. Her skin is pale as cream and freckled. Her eyes are a smoky shade of green, but she sometimes has to squeeze them when she particularly wants to see something. They aren't her most distinguishing feature.

"Pa needs him to help at the diggin's."

Liza looked disappointed for an instant, but then she brightened. I turned to look and saw the Wilson twins filling the doorway. I wouldn't have needed to actually look, for I could smell the cinnamon scent of the bakery on them.

I couldn't tell the two apart and I for sure didn't see how Liza managed, but she called out "Hi, Gus. Hi, Gunnar," as they clomped in. I suppose it was in the proper order. I always suspected they answered to either name, but they grinned and Liza 'most melted. I guessed she was confident she had sorted them out.

They jostled into place at the bench behind us just as Miss Jensen gave her bell a mighty shake. The first ring meant *Stand by your seat*. Liza and I stood at attention. The second ring meant *Be seated*. There was a last-minute scramble, then a rustling sound when the second bell rang and twenty bodies sank into place. The new school session was officially started.

Liza and I straightened as tall as we could stretch while sitting down. We all knew better than to be rude the first day.

Chapter 3

❖

MISS JENSEN called out the roll.

"Evangeline Stuart."

"Here, ma'am." Evangeline's pigtails swayed as she rose to her feet. Miss Jensen smiled at her and nodded, as if to say that Evangeline could sit down now that she had been counted. Evangeline sat down.

"Sarah Gustafson."

"Here, ma'am." Sarah jumped up from her place beside Evangeline and fidgeted for a second. She glanced over her shoulder and wrinkled her nose at Tony, then sat down again like a loose-limbed puppet.

The ritual was repeated over and over. No new kids had come, as far as I could see. Of course, I didn't dare to act like Sarah and turn around to look behind me. We older students were supposed to set an example.

"Liza McCutcheon."

Liza stood up and said, "Here, ma'am."

11

I was getting my legs ready to stand. Why is it that a person gets tensed up so just before her own turn? I was listening so hard for her to call out "Angelena Stuart" that I would have missed the excitement behind me except for Liza. She forgot about setting an example and twisted around to stare toward the door. For once, her eyes were round and wide open.

Rude or not, I turned, too.

In the doorway stood a woman and a girl. They each wore a quilted jacket that was the same color as their dark cloth shoes. Their calico skirts looked to be made from flour sacks.

The girl's head was bent. She seemed to be about my age, but that was the only thing we shared.

I'm a blonde; her hair was as black as a mine tunnel. I'm so fair-skinned that Mama says I sunburn by candle-light; her skin was the color of weak tea. My eyes are blue. When this girl finally raised her head, I saw that her eyes were like dark jewels in almond-shaped settings.

Miss Jensen didn't look at all surprised. She smiled and said, "Welcome," in a voice warm as quilts.

The girl smiled back in a gradual way, as if she were afraid someone would tell her to stop. Her teeth formed an even white crescent against dark skin. Plump cheeks rose high on her face, almost getting in the way of her eyes. She didn't speak.

The woman glanced up at Miss Jensen, then swiftly dropped her gaze to the floor again. "Excuse me." She spoke in a voice so low it was nearly a whisper. "They told me school starts today. I brought my so-stupid daughter so you can make her smart."

She put her hand on the girl's back and urged her forward. The girl took one faltering step.

A wave of subdued snickering pulsed through the back row, reminding me of the tiny birds we had heard that morning in the forest. Miss Jensen scowled it to a halt.

"Certainly. What is your daughter's name?"

The woman bent her head deeply in a sort of bow. "This is An Li."

"Angelena, our new student will sit next to you."

That wasn't the request I had prepared for. The second I heard my name, I jumped to my feet. "Here, ma'am."

More snickers. "I mean, yes, ma'am."

"Please show her where to put her things and make her feel welcome."

I kept my head down, too, as I passed the back row. The new girl leaned forward in a little bow that was like an echo of her mother's and followed me to the coatrack. I could hear her shoes swish against the wood floor as she took tiny steps behind me.

What should I say to her? We had lots of Chinese miners around Bounty, but I had never seen a Chinese woman or girl. Could she even speak English? I decided silence was my best choice and wordlessly led her to the bench I shared with Liza. When we were seated, Miss Jensen picked up her roll book.

"I think we need to find an American name for you to use at school. That way, it will be easier for you to make new friends. Is that all right?"

An Li didn't speak. She looked at the floor and held both hands clasped in front of her. I could see them squeeze each other as she nodded her head slightly.

"I think Leeana would be a nice name, don't you?"

The new girl's head barely moved down, then up a bit. Her eyes stayed focused on the floor. Her jaw muscles twitched, but she didn't say a word.

That is how I came to meet Leeana.

Chapter 4

❖

"I SAY WE NEED to pass a law to keep the Celestials out. There are too dang many of them and not enough jobs for real Americans in the first place."

Jasper spoke around a mouthful of apple pie. His cheeks bulged and bumped like a bagful of rabbits. His eyes glistened with pleasure and I wasn't sure if it was because of the pie or pure joy in the lecture he was delivering. Both pie and lectures were special favorites with him.

Jasper is Mama's younger brother. She half-raised him after their parents died, so he had lived with us most of my life. Last spring, he moved to a miner's cabin about a half mile up Bunkum Creek, but he still preferred Mama's cooking to his own. He usually ate with us. In exchange, he helped Pa some at the diggin's.

I knew better than to interrupt Jasper, but Tom chimed right in. "We tempted them to come over here in the first place. We promised them jobs and I guess we can't blame them for seeking gold once they're surrounded by it."

"There used to be a mighty grist of gold, but the big strikes on the Rogue are about played out. There isn't enough of anything to go around, these days. Not gold nor jobs. The only thing we have too much of is the dang Chinee."

Jasper was getting warmed up. I was used to his ways, and I expected he could go on straight through dessert and near to bedtime. There wasn't any other source of entertainment, so I stayed right still and listened.

"A Chinaman's fine to work over the tailings," Pa said quietly. "That's just leftovers anyway. No white man will work that hard for that little."

"Even tailings are too good for them. When a regular miner takes out the gold and leaves behind a pile of trash, that's just what it should stay . . . a pile of trash. I don't allow any dang Celestial to go through my house trash, so why should he make a living off my tailings? It just keeps them from going back where they belong."

Tom tried a bit of fence-mending. "Most of them want to go home. They just came here long enough to make some money and take it back to their families."

"Dang right. That's exactly the trouble with John Chinaman. He doesn't spend his money here. He sends it overseas to make China rich. Meanwhile, we have to fight for every single dang dollar!" Jasper punctuated each of his last three words by slamming his fist on the table.

Tom cut himself a second piece of pie and took a great bite. He chewed it as if it were a portion of Jasper's argument. After considerable chewing and thinking, he swallowed. "I hear they've got a famine over there. They need the money to buy food. It's plain wrong to prevent folks from eating, even if they do eat odd."

He looked sort of smug and self-righteous, as if he were about to take credit for all the kindness in the world. Then Pa made a statement that startled Tom.

"If they don't go home alive, they go home dead." He used his slow voice, the one that made people listen for sure. "I heard they bury the dead ones for a year or so, then dig 'em up and ship the bones back to China."

Tom gaped at Pa and then gulped down his most recent bite of pie with a gagging sound. Jasper's eyes narrowed as he watched Tom react, and I allow he was right to do so for the reaction was worth watching.

"Dis-GUSTIN'!" Tom put down his fork and pushed back from the table. "That's just disgustin'. Why, any decent man ought at least to stay buried!"

He abandoned his pie and stomped to the door, almost running me over where I stood quietlike beside the stove. He growled "disgustin'" one more time and went out, slamming the door so hard it made Pa laugh.

"Tom never could tolerate odd behavior. He thinks birds should stay in trees and snakes on the ground, the way creation was intended. Can't stand the idea of a flying snake, which is what those Chinese dragons amount to, I guess."

He laughed again and, with some considering, chose a piece of kindling out of the wood box. He peeled off a splinter and handed it to me with a twinkly smile. I put one end in the fire. When it supported a little flame, I handed it back and he carefully held the fire to his pipe bowl. The tobacco perfume joined the coffee's aroma and the heavy scent of our wood fire. It smelled like home.

Jasper watched this ritual as if it were entirely new to him, but I could see by the way his eyes went squinty and his jaw shifted that he was working up to another announcement. He took a big slurp of coffee and swallowed before he spoke.

"Tom's right. If they want to be buried in China so all-fired bad, they should go home and die there, so no one has to dig them up. It is disgustin' beyond belief for corpses to be gallivanting around in a jar."

Pa puffed out a cloud of smoke and shook his head. I shook my own, trying to imagine any dead person exactly gallivanting. Mama came close to the fire from settling the baby in his bed. She brushed her hands hard against the sides of her apron, as if to rub off anything that was less than pure.

"Now, Jasper, you just watch how you talk in front of my children. Other folks have other ways. Don't the Gustafsons eat odd sometimes? I couldn't believe when they offered us fish boiled in milk! And the McCutcheon clan eats sheep entrails! I could hardly keep my face arranged when Adelaide told me that."

She sat down in Tom's abandoned chair and gazed at his half-eaten pie for a moment before she picked up his fork and took a bite off the crust end. She sighed. "Still, we all work hard and we all manage to work together."

Jasper wouldn't be convinced to charity. "Those folks eat odd, but they look like regular Americans. Celestials are heathens who don't comprehend how to behave. They lie and steal and worship false gods in their dang joss house. They even put statues of their dang demons on the roof, and that's just plain inviting trouble. We'll all be better off when they're gone."

He banged his cup down. His chair squawked as he scraped it back. "I guess I'll go. I have to be up before dawn."

He stalked out of the door but, Mama being right there, he didn't slam it. I heard his voice mingle with Tom's for a minute, then the thump of his boots on the steps.

I sat in his empty chair. Jasper confused me. He was strong and handsome, and the girls giggled when he came around, but he was also angry lots of times.

"Why is he so all-fired upset? The Celestials aren't harming him personal, are they?"

Mama sighed, as she sometimes did when she considered Jasper. "Sometimes he just needs to let off steam."

She picked up her knitting and appeared to concentrate on her yarn and needles. Her lips moved slightly as she counted stitches and rows, then her hands fell into a rhythm of movement. The needles' regular *click-click-click* marked the passing minutes.

Pa drew on his pipe and closed his eyes. He wasn't asleep but his face was peaceful, like the baby's when he naps.

Mama's needles kept their steady pace. "Mrs. Gustafson said there is a little Chinese girl in town."

"Leeana. She's not so little. She sits with me and Liza."

"There aren't many Chinese children here. The men don't bring wives. I guess those people pay all kinds of respect to their ancestors, so any married man leaves his wife in China to take care of his parents. I admit, I admire the way they treat their families, but it must be lonely sometimes, not to have babies around."

Mama's voice wound softly around us, holding us together like the yarn passing over her needles.

"Does Leeana have brothers or sisters?"

"I don't know. I guess she doesn't, or they would have been in school, too."

"Well, I hope you can help her learn. I don't know how bright these people are, but I'm sure with your help she will do what she can."

Her needles marched across the row. She turned the work and marched them back. *Click-click. Click-click.*

I thought about Leeana and the way her eyes had stared fiercely at the pages of Miss Jensen's book about flowers and insects. I thought it would be too much for Leeana to start on, but she had set to with a will. There were lots of pictures, but they weren't pretty. Mostly they showed the spikes on bees' legs and the inside parts of blossoms. I would have helped her more if she had asked me. When Miss Jensen directed me to drill the second-graders on multiplication, I had left Leeana with Liza.

When I came back, Leeana was sitting on the very end of our bench with her feet almost in the aisle. Her hunched shoulders and arms formed a protective wall around the book on her lap. I glanced at Liza, but she just scowled and squinted at the book she had been assigned: *A History of the Roman Empire.*

I answered Mama, "I think she reads all right. It's hard to say. She doesn't talk much."

Lulled by the good smells and the regular tick of Mama's knitting, I soon grew heavy-eyed. I was entirely satisfied to snuggle under a pile of quilts and soak up Evangeline's warmth. I didn't hear Tom when he came in. I didn't notice when the fire burned low.

Morning found us plenty soon. Once again Mama filled the cabin with the rich smell of griddle cakes. Evangeline and I dressed and ate, and did our morning chores. Finally we set off for school. All that time, I didn't give Leeana another thought.

Chapter 5

❖

"Tarnation!"

I thought to chastise Evangeline for her cursing, but I shared her wonder at the ruckus in the school yard. A day of September sunshine had dried the thirsty earth, so at first it appeared that the two boys were having a dust fight. Snarls and groans coming from their direction convinced me, though, that more than dust was getting pounded. As near as I could tell from the size and noise of the crowd, they were well launched into their struggle and sprinting toward the finish.

"What is going on here?" We were so concentrated on the entertainment that we hadn't seen Miss Jensen come out of the schoolhouse. I might have missed her even then, except she was standing directly behind me when she spoke. She followed her question with a vigorous shaking of the bell and I made haste to step aside to let her by.

"Stop this nonsense right now!" She gave the bell

another shake. It seemed magical, the way the tight circle melted back. Two dusty boys were left behind, looking like the end of a hard day's haying.

Tony Gustafson appeared to have got the worst of the exchange. He lay spread out on his back with his eyes squeezed shut, spitting dust. One of the Wilson twins straddled him, leaning forward to pin Tony's arms to the ground above his head. The quiet of the crowd and noise of the bell affected them like cold water. They scrambled up and stood side by side to face Miss Jensen, and whatever doom she planned for them.

"Explain yourselves." She looked fierce as poison oak to me, but I can't say if they thought the same. Both of those boys were a head taller than Miss Jensen. She had to bend her neck back a good amount to get them in her sights. Still, Tony studied his feet as if he had just discovered he owned a pair of them.

The Wilson twin muttered, "It wasn't nothing, ma'am. We were just foolin' around and I suppose it looked real mean, but it wasn't."

"Tony?" Her voice was a bit taller than she was.

"Yes, ma'am. We weren't wrathy. We were only foolin'."

"Then shake hands like gentlemen and come inside." She started for the door, then turned back as if she had just thought of something. "And for goodness sake, brush off that dirt. I just swept the floor."

She led the way into the school and we followed as slowly as we dared. Evangeline held my hand going up the steps. She wasn't quite so used to school goings-on as I was.

While we hung up our sweaters, Liza leaned toward me and whispered, but if she wanted to share a secret she'd picked the wrong place and time. In that quiet room she was loud as a rooster at sunrise.

"I allow that will teach Tony Gustafson to stick up for the dang Celestials."

I glanced around, seeking out Leeana and wondering if she had heard. She was nowhere in sight. We were at our seats and opening our books for quiet reading when the *swish* sound of her shoes and a soft motion on my right told me she had arrived. She didn't say a word, just opened her book and stared at it. I watched her kind of sideways. She turned the pages at such a steady rate that I figured maybe she didn't understand at all. She didn't ask for help, though.

It was quiet reading time, but Liza whispered, "Angelena." She looked merry. "I brought us a treat." She gestured back toward the lunch pails.

That increased my interest a good bit. Mrs. McCutcheon made the best pound cake in Bounty and I dared to hope that was the nature of the treat. As soon as Miss Jensen dismissed us, Liza bounced up and grabbed my sleeve. She pulled me along as she scooted to the left end of our bench, the end away from Leeana.

Liza's mother knew I was greatly partial to pound cake and she had packed a powerful amount. Liza gave a slice to each of the Wilson boys and even included

Tony. Then she hastened me to our private place under the oak.

There was more to the treat than cake, if Liza's manner was a clue to her intentions. Finally she could contain her secret no longer and burst forth with it.

"I have the grandest news! There's going to be a picnic party and we're all to be invited." She nearly floated in the air, she was so full of plans and expectations.

It seemed that Charlie, the oldest Gustafson boy, was courting a girl from the stagehouse up at Golden. The girl didn't consider it proper to go out with him alone, so he was getting a riding party together. The plan was to leave right early on Sunday and get to Golden by midmorning. We could share a picnic, have all sorts of entertainments, and be home again by dark.

"Mother will surely let me go if she knows you're going, too, Angelena."

It did sound like a good time. Charlie was eighteen, old enough to be serious about courting. He and Mr. Gustafson worked a claim past Pa's down Bunkum Creek. I guessed he would likely invite Tom, and that made me extra hopeful that Mama might let me go. I was nearly courting age myself, though I had never met a fellow who held my interest. A riding party sounded like pure joy.

"Do you think they'll ask Tom? If they do, maybe Mama will let me go, even though it is on Sunday."

"Tom must surely come. No one is left out." From the way she patted her hair I figured Liza had already

25

counted up the group and Tom was, for sure, included in the total.

"I'll ask Mama. I guess I could get out of chores for just one day, and Evangeline can watch the baby."

Feeling so full of plans made me generous with the joy. Without thinking, I added, "Leeana will get to meet everyone, too."

Liza's face went from peart to prunish. "This is a picnic party, Angelena. It's for regular Americans. It is not for ignorant heathens, who wouldn't understand how to act proper in civilized company."

She glared past my shoulder. When I turned to look, I wasn't surprised to see Leeana sitting on the schoolhouse steps. She looked alone as a hummingbird in wintertime.

"Come on, Liza. She's new here, is all. She isn't hurting anyone."

"She *is* hurting someone! Anyway her mother is. The Wilsons' dad says her mom hasn't been in town a month and already she's making baked goods and delivering them right to the mining camps. That cuts into his business."

"Well," I said, drawing it out as grown-up sounding as I could, "I would think with two sons big enough to whup Tony Gustafson, Mr. Wilson could arrange to deliver baked goods himself."

"Not to the mining camps." Liza said it head-high and final. "Not to those Chinamen out in the woods.

They worship devils, you know. An American probably wouldn't get back to town with his whole skin intact."

"That's nonsense, Liza. No one would worship devils! The Chinese are just like any miners, digging all the long day and yearning for a big strike. Except they yearn for their families, too, left behind in China." I thought I put that pretty fancy and was glad for hearing the conversation around the table the night before.

"That old China boss, Gin Lin, goes home all right, but he doesn't stay put. He keeps coming back, and every time he brings a new wife! I hear he sells the leftovers. Chinese do that, you know. They sell their women worse than slaves, and we all know it isn't proper to own slaves. We had a war to prove that."

I had no answer. I had heard the stories, too, of the man who brought a new wife from China every time he went home to visit. The old wives, the ones sold into slavery, were rumored to be scattered all around the gold country, but I had never actually seen one. I suspicioned it was just stories.

Unless . . . could it be that Leeana's mother was one of them? The image of her bowed head and low voice fit with someone who lived as a slave. I glanced back at Leeana. Instead of seeming shy, I allowed she might act so quiet because she was forced to keep humble. How would it feel to be the daughter of a slave? I was still trying to sort that out when the bell clanged, calling us inside.

Chapter 6

❖

AFTER LUNCH it was time for "pairs." We older kids were put to work helping the littler ones. I was assigned to Evangeline, who was just beginning to write her letters in cursive.

We hardly ever used paper in our school. It was far too dear. Each of us had a piece of slate to write on and the black-painted chalkboard was for general lessons. Letter practice worked best in sand.

The sand table stood next to a window where the light was good. Its sides were raised a bit, making the top a shallow box that held a thin layer of sand. Beginning writers traced out letters, then spread the sand smooth and started over.

Miss Jensen said it helped them learn if they could feel the letters while they looked at them. I was special fond of the *swish-swish* sound of sand grains scraping against one another to make alphabets, and sometimes whole words.

I guided Evangeline's finger to make the first five capital letters. Then she wiped away *A, B, C, D,* and *E* with her palm and went on from *F.* She went all the way through *Z* and started the little letters. We had done this before, and I admit my attention wandered.

I glanced out the window at the empty school yard and the road up Cemetery Hill. Toward the back of the room Leeana hunched over her book as if she were all taken up with what she was reading. Except, the pages weren't turning. Her face was hidden, but I knew from my own tricks that she could be looking 'most anywhere. I also knew she couldn't see the Wilson boys directly behind her.

Gus and Gunnar were busy-seeming at their numbers, but the smiles snaking across their faces said to me it wasn't working numbers that had them so proud. One of them glanced toward Miss Jensen's desk. He must have been satisfied that he was safe, for he raised his two index fingers and pulled his eyes all slanty. At the same time he pulled his lips back with his thumbs and waggled his tongue like a fool. A chorus of smothered giggles and strangled-sounding coughs rewarded him. His hands were down and his face all put back together by the time Miss Jensen called for order.

Liza had twisted in her seat to admire his performance. She turned to face front with her hand covering her mouth and her eyes bright with laughter. She looked right at me for a second and I admit her merriment acted like a magnet. It pulled an answering smile across my face, and even a snorting sort of giggle.

I told myself I was laughing at Liza, not Leeana, but it would have been easy to misunderstand. I covered the giggle with a cough and concentrated on Evangeline. She was all the way to little *m*.

Directly after Miss Jensen dismissed us that afternoon, I saw the Wilson boys whispering with Liza. I tried to ignore them, but allow that part of me wished to be included in their whispering. Liza was my life-long friend and it felt odd to think she was sharing secrets with someone else.

I hung back, fussing with my sweater so I wouldn't have to walk past them and chance not being invited to join in. I watched them with their heads together until one of the Wilson boys laughed, loud as a donkey, and they both ran off.

"What's that about?" I walked toward Liza casual-like.

"Why, it was only more plans for the picnic." She acted silky as cream. "Do you think Evangeline will do your chores so you can come along?"

It wasn't exactly a change of subject, but it kept me from asking more questions. I was even more distracted when I looked for Evangeline. She was nowhere in sight.

The Gustafsons always dashed directly home, for their mother was extra strict about lingering. Evangeline might have gone with Sarah, but she knew she was supposed to wait for me. I mumbled a quick good-bye to Liza and headed down Main Street. Up ahead, I saw Tony, Mae, George, and Sarah, but Evangeline was not with them.

"She must be playing some hide-and-seek game," I muttered out loud, hoping I wouldn't find her peering into the gambling saloon.

She wasn't there. As far as I could see, she wasn't anywhere. I spied behind the shrubs and sheds, and peeked around the edge of the boardinghouse. I looked down Apple Street where our church stands, sedate as an old lady. 'Most to the center of town, I looked for her. Then I gave off simple looking and started an earnest search back along the creek toward the school.

Bunkum Creek borders the east side of Bounty. The creek is narrow and water flows swiftly under the plank bridge, but upstream by the school it is walk-across shallow. Evangeline had a special liking for the dragonflies that tatted the air above the gentle waters of midsummer. It might be that she had wandered in search of late-season dragonflies.

I tried to keep close to the water's edge, but willow trees crowded the bank and kept me back. Then, above the whisper of water on rock, I heard a cry of fear.

Chapter 7

❖

I PUSHED right through the underbrush, heading bee-line straight for the sound. I came out at an open place where water, eddying around a boulder, had left deposits of sand. Evangeline stood on that beach, face-to-face with a bobcat.

Maybe he had been napping away daylight beside the stream, or maybe he had come to drink. Either way, Evangeline had blundered into his territory and he took exception to her being there.

This cat was big, at least twice the size of our Old Tom. He was powerful large to start, then piled on the agony by swelling himself to enormous. He arranged himself sideways to Evangeline and stood stiff-legged, arching his back, and raising his hair into a bushy halo. I reckon my fear added some to his size, too.

His dark eyes were arrows pointed at Evangeline's heart and his dagger teeth glistened. Evangeline shifted her weight as if to pull foot out of there. The bobcat hissed. It was a standoff.

The creek flowed behind the cat. The boulder blocked his way on the downstream side. Upstream, a willow thicket crowded the water's edge. The natural way to freedom was across the sandy stretch and up the bank, but that way was blocked by my little sister. Time seemed to pause. None of us moved, not a breath or a flicker.

Then a blur of activity broke the spell and time jumped forward. I had a quick impression of night-dark hair and Oriental eyes. It was Leeana, and those eyes held fire. She planted herself firmly between Evangeline and the cat.

This was not the shy girl who sat beside me at school. This girl was more like demons I had heard of in tales.

Shielding Evangeline with her body, Leeana faced the cat. She spoke to it, crooning in a low, soothing tone. The cat's eyes shifted from Evangeline and fastened on Leeana. Ever so slowly, nudging my sister along behind her, Leeana backed away. Evangeline took three halting, backward steps, then turned and fled into my arms. I held her ever so close while Leeana continued her slow-motion retreat. The bobcat watched her for another moment, then undertook a retreat of its own, dodging up the bank and out of sight.

"You saved us a lot of grief." Evangeline had stopped trembling and was breathing small and steady once again. "We're both grateful." It sounded stiff, but I couldn't find any better words.

"Wasn't anything but common sense. It wasn't as serious as it looked, anyway. That old bobcat could have gone right through the creek anytime. He was just too lazy to get his feet wet."

She looked me right in the eye when she spoke with her face turned into the sunlight, as if someone had tied a string to her chin and pulled upward. Something else was different, too. When Leeana wasn't whispering, she sounded just like anyone else.

"Common sense, maybe," I told her, "but it was brave, too. I wouldn't move toward a scared bobcat. It's more sensible to go the other way."

"Your sister couldn't decide. I just helped her out."

"I was too scared to decide anything," Evangeline said. Without hesitating, she slipped her hand into Leeana's. The look on her face said "Thanks" better than any words I had to offer.

Feeling extra glad to have her safe, I took Evangeline's other hand. It felt natural as anything for the three of us to walk through town that way.

"I didn't know you could talk English so well," Evangeline said. "I never heard you say much, I guess."

Leeana shrugged. "My mother and my old teacher make me use English. They say I have to be able to get along with everyone."

Evangeline and I had two choices about how to get home. We could cross the plank bridge in town

34

and take the wide trace through the woods past the Gustafsons', or we could keep going right down Main Street to the south part of Bounty. That way took us through China Shacks, where the Celestials lived. At the far edge of China Shacks was a big log we could use to cross Bunkum Creek.

It wasn't exactly hard to cross on the log, but it wasn't as safe as the real bridge. Once across it, though, we only had to climb the hill and we would be home. The way through China Shacks was shorter, but because of the log bridge and maybe because of the strangers who lived there, Mama preferred for us to go the long way. I usually preferred it, too.

I figured that day was an exception. It was simple politeness to walk Leeana home. As we went down Main Street, Evangeline stayed, safe and chattery, between us. She didn't notice Mrs. Wilson staring at us from inside the bakery.

We proceeded past the bank and general store and Johnson's livery stable at the edge of town. Old Mr. Johnson looked a mite surprised to see us in company with a Celestial, I guess, but he returned Evangeline's wave with a salute.

Leeana kept her head bowed a bit, modestlike, and didn't wave at all. I began to realize she didn't mean any rudeness by not looking at folks. That was proper company manners to her. She didn't get overfamiliar with strangers. I was grateful to conclude that she didn't view a bobcat as a stranger.

Past the livery we entered China Shacks. Tiny plank houses clustered so close they seemed to be leaning on each other. A few shared an outside wall, so the straight-up truth was that they weren't really separate houses at all. I guessed shacks was the proper word to use, even if it didn't sound exactly charitable.

On our left, the Chinese washhouse perched beside Bunkum Creek. A pile of buckets dripped creek water beside the open front door. Inside I could just make out two moving figures. I was curious to see more, but it was Evangeline who rushed forward to peer at the laundrymen. I was afraid of her being impolite, but Leeana followed and Evangeline turned to beckon me.

"Angelena, come take a gander at this!"

I took her advice and went to look.

Inside, two Chinese men worked fast as fiddlers. One stirred a vat of hot water and dirty clothes with a paddle that looked like a small boat oar. His bony shoulders didn't look like he had strength to lift a kitten, but the water did go round and round, and he even dragged up extra energy to chatter at his friend.

To my ear it was just whoops and groans, but Leeana must have understood, for she laughed at something he said. It sounded to me as if jaybirds had been teaching language to the Celestials. It was all punctuation marks and no spelling.

The second man was in no danger of talking back, and for the strangest reason: he was spitting on the clothes! He grasped a heavy-looking copper pan by its long wood handle. Smoke rose from the pan, and it looked so much like Mama's bed warmer that I guessed it must hold live embers. He moved like liquid as he stretched and leaned forward, passing the hot copper bottom across a shirt that was spread before him on a big, padded table.

Then he set down the pan and picked up a shallow dish filled with water. Tilting his head back, he filled his mouth. My first idea was that he was thirsty, but he never swallowed. With his cheeks bulging out, he picked up the ironing pan again, leaned over, and spit an even spray across that shirt.

All the while, calm as you please, he worked his copper pan back and forth. It just took a moment to iron the shirt smooth as glass. Mama would surely have admired the shirt, but I didn't expect to see her spitting on our laundry any time soon.

I forgot my manners when I saw him spit and gasped out loud. He glanced our way and his eyebrows rose, then his eyes found Leeana, and he smiled a careful greeting. I was powerful glad he didn't try to say hello.

Leeana bowed a little and Evangeline copied her. I tried on a smile that I hope was respectful, and we hastened on our way.

Scents that hinted of faraway swept over us like a river, pulling us deeper into China Shacks. There was a strong flower smell that I did recognize as incense from the times I passed the Catholic church on Sundays.

Leeana hurried us past one crooked shack that had no windows. I breathed in a sharp, sweet smell that was entirely new to me. Her bustling and the way she looked in the other direction told me this must be some Celestial version of a gambling saloon.

I reached for Evangeline's hand again. She kept extra close and I was glad for that. She was the only thing within my reach that was perfectly ordinary and familiar.

Boom! We both flinched. *Boom! Boom!* It wasn't exactly music, but I determined it was a drum. Three times more it sounded, this time in company with a thunderous deep note. The drum and gong sounded together . . . one, two, three times.

Chapter 8

❖

"Where did that come from?" Evangeline dropped my hand and turned in a full circle, trying to locate the source of the sound.

Leeana pointed down a short side street. "It's from the joss house. Someone is calling the gods to hear a prayer."

Evangeline pursed her lips. "You mean it's like church bells?"

"I reckon so. It's supposed to get the gods' attention."

Evangeline considered that. "Miss Jensen rings a bell, too, when she wants *our* attention."

Evangeline looked satisfied, but I didn't entirely share her satisfaction. Twice Leeana had mentioned gods. I had been taught there was only one God.

Every Sunday, my whole family and most of our neighbors go to our church in the village. The Catholics have their own church, a little farther down Apple Street. Our building is simple-plain; the Catholics have some colored glass in the side windows, and a bell in a tower. Mostly, though, it's plain, too. Neither of them is anything like the place where Leeana's people worshiped.

The joss house was a confusion of opposites. It was a long way from being a shack. It was made of planks, and it stood properlike behind a tidy white picket fence. In those ways, it was the same as any of Bounty's most genteel establishments. Everything else about it was surprising as an August rain.

Carved dragonfish perched on the roof peak, crouching face-to-face like two unacquainted cats. Swooping red beams, all carved and curlicued, outlined the steep roof. They swept down, then up again, ending in sharp points.

Our church is painted white all over, and the porch matches the rest of the building. The joss house was white, too, but its entryway was bright blue. Close-up I could see lines drawn over blue paint to make a kind of grid, as if someone wanted people to think it was really blue tiles set on the wall.

I was right aware of Leeana, who stood directly behind us, holding silent. I thought she must be waiting to see how we reacted to her temple. Mama always told me, "Honesty is the best policy." The trouble was, I wasn't positive what my honest opinion might be.

"It's beautiful." My words sounded wrong. It wasn't beautiful like a rose or a mountain. I tried again. "It's beautiful, but it's odd."

"Are those the gods someone was calling?"

Sometimes I'm glad for Evangeline's habit of interrupting. She stared up at the dragonfish with her jaw shifting very slightly from side to side, as if she were considering possibilities.

They for sure didn't resemble the white-bearded figure I imagined when I thought about God. I was afraid she was fixing to put in a request, maybe ask the dragonfish for a new kitten or a pony.

Leeana spoke before Evangeline could commit that folly. "No, they aren't exactly gods. They are friendly spirits who protect against fire. The old temple burned so the uncles insisted on these spirit carvings to protect the new one."

She squinted up toward the joss house's roof, which was a marvel of carving and folderol. "The roof edges are curved and pointed to keep evil spirits out. They slide right off."

Evangeline looked startled and stared at the joss house roof as if she could imagine a crowd of demons using it as a kind of slippery slide. Leeana smiled in a way that made me wonder for a moment if she might be laughing at us for our ignorance. Still, she sounded sincere when she went on explaining.

"Evil spirits can only roll in straight lines. That's why the gate isn't directly across from the entrance. The demons have to make a turn and they won't do it. That's also the reason we make the threshold so high."

"Do you *really* believe in demons and such?" Evangeline's voice was hushed and excited, both. We had never heard anything about rolling demons in our Sunday school!

Leeana's answer came quick and definite. "I believe in spirits. I believe some are friendly and some are not friendly. It makes sense to be careful."

A sound drew her attention to the joss house and a smile overflowed her face. She called to two men coming out. "Hello, Uncles."

A tiny man, tiny even for a Celestial, blinked as he came into the sunlight. He turned to help his companion. This man had hair so white it almost glowed and his face reminded me of the dried apple dolls Evangeline and I made during harvest. He spoke breathlessly as he stepped with brittle care over the high doorsill.

I couldn't understand his words, but the two of them appeared to be at odds about something. Their voices held an arguing tone that would have horrified Mama, especially since they were coming out of a sacred building. Leeana called out again and they looked our way. The rain clouds of argument gave way to sunny expressions.

"Niece, have you brought us young visitors?" The older man held his arms wide as if he intended to embrace all three of us. His wrinkled face was all smiles and echoes of smiles, but still he scared me a little. My family isn't great shakes on hugging strangers, but more

42

than that I was startled to see the three middle fingers of his right hand were entirely gone.

I must have looked as shy as Leeana when her mother first brought her to our school. I studied my feet while Leeana introduced us.

"Uncles, these are my new friends, Evangeline and Angelena Stuart. They are walking home with me." She elbowed me very gently, and I looked up.

They bowed deeply, all the while looking as pleased as cats in a sunbeam. "Welcome, welcome. We are glad to meet you, very much glad."

Leeana called the older man, the one with the missing fingers, Uncle Shoon. I had seen the younger man around town. Everyone I knew called him China Joe, but Leeana called him Uncle Chou. It sounded almost like Uncle Joe.

China Joe studied me and Evangeline thoughtfully, then exclaimed, "Two angels! We are favored with much good fortune today." He looked pleased with his gentle joke and I was amazed. Most people, even ones who speak good English, didn't notice the "angel" in our names.

"You're lucky to have two uncles," I said, thinking of the difference between these smiling men and Jasper.

"It's a title we use to show respect," Leeana said. "But Uncle Shoon really is related to me. The way you count it, he is my great-uncle. My mother is his niece."

Uncle Shoon nodded agreement and put his arm around Leeana's shoulders. She didn't seem to notice his injured hand at all. I tried not to let him see me cringe.

Evangeline bowed first to China Joe and then to Uncle Shoon. "Pleased to meet you. Whatever happened to your hand?"

Leeana answered quickly. "He was carrying an ax and he fell."

Uncle Shoon regarded Evangeline with his head tilted, as if he were memorizing her. Finally he said, "Yes, Second Angel. So from this you must learn always to be careful with axes."

Evangeline seemed content, but I wondered if Leeana had told the exact truth. When she kept her face so still it was hard to read her meaning.

China Joe was thin as a garter snake, and he was snake-graceful, too. He stood right at eye level with me, and Uncle Shoon was only a frog's hair taller. They were dressed about like anybody, except they wore cloth shoes, like Leeana's, and on their heads they wore black felt hats. I knew from rumor that they would have long braids coiled up under those hats.

We all walked together back to Main Street. The uncles shouted quick Chinese to each other, now and then stopping to say a few words in English to me and Evangeline. I reckoned their recipe for conversation was equal parts spit and laughter. Their argument had vanished without a trace as far as I could tell, and I began to realize it was the nattering of friends, sort of like when Liza and I had a discussion about which boy was sweet on which girl. It was more of an entertainment than a disagreement.

We stopped in front of Sam Wise's grocery. It was a building like the stores in the main section of Bounty: made of brick and two stories tall. Iron shutters on each side of the big front windows stood open, so we could examine what Sam Wise had for sale.

I'm afraid Evangeline and I were rude, for we planted foot in front of that window and just stared. There were metal boxes that I figured must hold tea, and odd-shaped brown ceramic jars, some with a tiny spout coming out of the side.

A small sign propped in the window said: SAM WISE: DRY GOODS AND GROCERIES. Over the door was a big sign with writing made of dots and curving crossed lines. I didn't see how anyone could ever learn to read a language made of signs instead of letters.

Leeana and Uncle Shoon stayed with us while China Joe excused himself. "A thousand pardons, but I have business here." He went inside.

"He's a beekeeper," Uncle Shoon explained. "In the Pearl River valley, where we come from, his family has raised bees for many generations. Bees make the trees give very much fruit and Chou's bees make honey better even than gold. It must be so, for why else would miners trade gold for honey?" He wheezed laughter.

We could see China Joe talking to Sam Wise; then Sam counted money into his outstretched hand. At least they acted as if it was money, but even at a distance I could tell it wasn't American cash at all. It was paper with the same kind of strange Chinese writing as the sign above Sam's door.

Uncle Shoon saw my puzzlement. "We use Chinese money between ourselves. We understand Chinese money better."

He plucked a round metal disk from his pocket and held it up between his left thumb and forefinger. It was a dull, brass color and had a square hole in the center.

"It's all the same. Money for sweet, sweet for money. You wait here. Chinese money works. I'll show you."

He dashed through the door and spoke briefly to Sam. When he came out, he held his closed left hand close to his chest.

"A bit of sweet for An Li's honored friends."

With a dramatic flourish, he extended his arm toward Evangeline and opened his hand. In it lay three pieces of candy, each one wrapped in paper.

She took one without hesitation. "Thank you," she said prettily.

He offered the candy to me next. "First Angel?"

I took one piece and whispered, "Thank you."

He beamed. "You sound like a Chinese girl. Very good manners. Very good. An Li could learn from you."

That caused me some astonishment, because I thought Leeana's manners were about perfect. She just naturally seemed to know that the proper way to act was to be shy as a baby bird around all of her elders, especially teachers and strangers.

Then I thought of how she had faced down that cat. She just naturally seemed to know a bobcat's idea of manners, too.

She was watching me. I bowed to Uncle Shoon again, extra respectful. He laughed out loud and I caught Leeana's eye. She was smiling, friendly as sunshine.

The candy melted slowly and filled my mouth with plum sweetness. It had been sweet, too, to hear the word "friends" from Leeana's uncle. I felt like I was being welcomed into another land right inside my own hometown.

We strolled farther down Main Street, leaving the old gentlemen in front of the grocery. Their voices were raised again, only this time the noise was considerably increased, for Sam Wise had joined in the discussion. I knew by then that the argument was for fun, not for serious, and I even felt a little happy at the sound of them enjoying each other's opinions.

I was some relieved to see that Leeana's place was more like a real house than a shack. It had glass windows guarded by iron shutters, like Sam Wise's grocery. Inside, the windows were covered with calico curtains.

Mrs. Lee (for that is what she said we should call her) came out on the porch to greet us, wiping her hands on her apron with the same gesture I had seen Mama use a thousand times.

"You will stay for fresh sweet buns?" Her smile took over her face to such a degree that her eyes nearly closed.

I reckon Evangeline wanted to go in and see the house, but we both knew that we mustn't tarry. "Thank you, ma'am," I told her, "but we can't stay. Mama will be needing us to do chores."

It took just a few minutes to cross the log bridge back into familiar territory. Climbing the hill to home, I felt like I had passed some kind of test.

Chapter 9

❖

"SHE WAS JUST FULL of grit, Mama. She faced that old bobcat and told him to skedaddle out of there and—bang!—sure enough he did skedaddle. She wasn't scared a bit."

Evangeline pulled in a deep breath. Her heels tattooed against the rungs of her chair as she spoke, like drums telling the story.

Mama looked at me. "Did she really face down a bobcat?"

I nodded, but seeing the worry enter her eyes, I thought to make less of the story than Evangeline had. "He wasn't really cornered, though. He could have crossed the creek any old time. Evangeline sort of took him by surprise and they were looking each other over when I got there." I omitted to explain how all-fired scared *I* had been.

She relaxed a little. "Well, in the future, I want you girls to stay together. You don't have Tom around to look after you. There could be bigger cats, like cougar, or bears, or even rattlers. You need to watch out for each other."

She turned back to the stove and I gave Evangeline a warning glance. No need to trouble Mama over things we could handle on our own. We hastened out to feed old Turnip and Majesty and load fresh firewood in the bin beside the stove.

When we set out for school the next morning, Evangeline didn't even glance at the trail past the Gustafsons'. She headed directly down the steep path toward the log bridge and China Shacks. I followed right willingly.

I think we could have found Leeana's house with our eyes closed for the fresh-baked perfume reached all the way to the creek. Most of the Celestials' shacks didn't have chimneys, but Mrs. Lee must have needed a western-style stove to bake her special buns. Smoke rose from a pipe through their roof.

Leeana was at the window. She fluttered her hand in greeting and disappeared. That window, like most things in China Shacks, was a puzzle to me. The ruffled curtains inside didn't fit with the iron shutters outside. I knew folks had used such shutters to protect their houses during the Rogue Indian War, but that was long ago. I had seen them at the grocery and a few other buildings in China Shacks, but never anywhere else in Bounty.

Other than the shutters, Leeana's house was ordinary enough. Mama would have approved of that clean-swept porch. Evangeline clearly approved of the sweet-looking burro tied to its railing. She crooned and stroked the burro's velvety gray neck while he blinked enormous eyes.

Leeana stepped out and held the door for her mother, who came out with a basket brimming with fragrant buns. They were wrapped in flour-sack fabric. Steam rose in tendrils that carried the delicate scent.

Mrs. Lee put the basket down and bowed toward us. "So here are the little angels. Welcome to our home. Are you hungry?"

I saw Evangeline eyeing the basket and hastened to say, "No, thank you, Mrs. Lee. We just had griddle cakes at home."

"Maybe you will stop after school. I will prepare a treat." Her dark eyes nearly matched Leeana's.

"Yes, ma'am." It seemed the polite thing to say, and I'll admit a treat sounded good, even though I was full of griddle cakes right then.

"Let me help you," Leeana said, but her mother gently refused. "Uncle will help. You go and get education with your friends."

Friends. The word was beginning to feel comfortable, especially in combination with the smiles and good smells and in the company of the big-eyed burro.

"Hello, Angels!" Uncle Shoon approached slowly, limping a bit as he walked. He put his left hand on Leeana's head, mussing her hair in a way that would have caused me some aggravation.

Leeana hugged him. "How are you this morning, Uncle?"

"My bones feel old today. I'm like a lizard. I need to warm up before I can run after grasshoppers. Don't worry, though. Once I'm warm, I catch plenty."

His face was as wrinkled as crumpled paper, but the grin folded up in there suggested that he would fancy grasshopper chasing. Stooping, he picked up the loaded basket and very slowly straightened. Leeana's mother helped him to position it on one side of the burro.

The burro ignored them. He was enjoying Evangeline's affection and appeared to have no interest in anything else.

Mrs. Lee held the basket in place while Uncle Shoon tied it securely with a piece of rope. I couldn't keep from staring as he used just his thumb and little finger to do the work of a whole hand.

When they had finished the job to Mrs. Lee's satisfaction, she stepped back and brushed her hands on her apron. "The miners will be hungry. Uncle will go to the mining camps. I'll bake more buns. You go to school."

"Yes, ma'am." Leeana's tone was obedient.

I started to leave, but Mrs. Lee appeared not to be quite ready to let Leeana go. She whispered to her in Chinese. Her words sounded entirely strange, but her manner was a lot like Mama's when she gave me last-minute advice. She repaired the mussing Uncle Shoon had inflicted on Leeana's hair, then brushed lint from her quilted jacket. The straight-up truth is, I couldn't see any slightest sign of lint.

None of this delay fussed Evangeline at all. She just

kept talking to that burro. They were getting past early acquaintance and were progressing toward long-term friendship. At last she felt a need to be introduced.

"What's his name?"

Mrs. Lee beamed at her. "His name is a joke. We bought him from a dairy farmer, so we call him Buttermilk." Her wheezed laughter sounded just like her uncle's.

Uncle Shoon made soft clicking sounds to coax Buttermilk along. A day's work started before dawn on the gravel bars, and miners would have built up a good appetite already. Uncle Shoon and his basket of warm buns would be welcome.

He waved to us as he set off, still limping. I worried some about him, but Leeana said he would take his time going out and ride Buttermilk on the trip home.

"His hip was hurt a long time ago. He's used to walking slowly."

I feared we would have to pull foot to get to school on time and wanted to rush through China Shacks, but the sights and sounds made it hard to hurry. There weren't a lot of Celestials around, but those we saw wanted us to stop and say hello. Mostly, the men who stayed in town were too old or too crippled to do the hard work of mining. The younger men camped out at their diggin's so as not to miss a minute of daylight.

Leeana said the men were lonely, remembering families and children they had left behind. For them, the most important thing in life was family, but in this land that was home for me, they were strangers, traveling alone.

Sam Wise fussed over a bin of apples in front of his grocery. At the washhouse, the two laundrymen were at work: one stirring and chattering and the other spitting water on clean clothes. I came to the realization that the only woman in all of China Shacks was Leeana's mother, and Leeana was the only Chinese child.

Once past Mr. Johnson's livery, we did hasten. I didn't even glance at the gambling saloon. Right ahead past Wilson's Bakery, I saw Miss Jensen standing on the schoolhouse porch. Her bell was ready in her hand.

Liza was hurrying, too, coming from the other direction. I waved at her and called out. She was looking toward me, but I thought she must not have seen, for she turned away.

Evangeline had run ahead. Leeana drifted back. I discovered myself alone at the edge of the school yard. I felt confused, for no one looked at me or said anything, as if I had become invisible. I came to understand why Leeana came to school at the last minute. The school yard wasn't a friendly place if you were almond-eyed, or if you were with someone who was almond-eyed.

When Leeana did enter the school yard, she became the shy Chinese girl who walked with tiny steps and looked at her feet more than the landscape. It was hard to believe that she was the same girl who laughed with old men and shooed away bobcats.

Liza acted like sour milk. She stood in a cluster

with Gus and Gunnar, keeping her back toward me. When Miss Jensen's bell rang, Liza rushed in with unaccustomed haste. At the second bell, she plopped down, ignoring me as if I were a chunk of granite rock. I didn't dare to whisper loudly, but I tried to tell her good morning. She stared hard at her book. I got a little stubborn then and stared at my book, too.

Just before lunch, Miss Jensen asked Leeana to come up to her desk for questions about her reading. I took the chance to whisper to Liza. "I brought cinnamon rolls."

Her eyes flickered up just once, but I knew she was ready to be friends again. Liza has a forgiving nature, and I knew she loved Mama's cinnamon rolls as much as I loved her mother's pound cake. When the lunch bell rang, she allowed me to lead her out to the big oak.

Liza seemed inclined to forget my offense, and I knew from past experiences that the forgiveness game was special to her heart. I didn't mind much, once I was used to it. The cold, angry part never lasted long, and the making up felt fine. I was just glad to be friends again.

"Well, can you go?" She was breathless at the prospect of our riding picnic. Of course I was right aware that she couldn't stay mad at me and expect to see much of Tom.

"Mama said it would be fine if I would only spend a bit of extra time on my Bible reading to make up for missing church on Sunday." I waited to see what Liza would say about the Bible reading, feeling a mixture of reluctance for the burden and satisfaction for the holiness.

She didn't notice. "Good. We'll all meet at Wilson's Bakery right after breakfast. Gus and Gunnar are going, too."

She looked so pleased that I feared for the boys' tranquillity. Liza liked having one fellow well enough, but she adored having more than one. She knew how jealousy could spur on a suitor.

We talked some more about the plans for Sunday, with Liza confident as birdsong that we would have good weather. She told me how her sister, Belle, had promised to braid her hair in "that fancy new French style."

"Is Belle coming with us?" Tom had asked special, but I didn't mention who wanted to know. It might have spoiled Liza's mood.

"Oh, yes, just everyone is coming. It will be a real party." She chattered on and I reminded myself to tell Tom to expect Belle's company.

Miss Jensen had asked Leeana to stay back, most likely for extra help. Now she came out, blinking in the sunlight. As I watched her step over the high doorsill, I was reminded of the joss house's elevated threshold, designed to keep mean spirits away.

Leeana didn't look happy, and I thought how shamed she must be to have trouble reading. I had a time catching her eye, for she stubbornly looked everywhere but at me and Liza. When at last she glanced our way, I waved her over.

"Come on, Leeana. I saved one for you." I held up the third cinnamon roll to tempt her over.

"Are you crazy?" Liza hissed. "They'll all think you're a white Chinee."

"I'm not any kind of Chinee. I'm just trying to be Leeana's friend."

There. I had said it aloud. I swallowed any doubts and gazed firm-eyed at Liza.

The word "friend" was apparently a mite strong for her peace of mind. "Then you're not mine!" She threw her half-eaten roll on the dusty ground and stomped off.

I wanted to call after her, but I knew everyone would hear and guess what we had been arguing about. Especially Leeana would hear and guess. I stayed still and watched Liza go.

Leeana watched, too. I beckoned again, and it hurt to see her hesitate. Finally, she crossed the school yard and sat on the warm ground beside me. She spoke quietlike, with her hands clasped and her eyes avoiding mine.

"Maybe it's better for you if they don't see us together."

"That just isn't so." I tried to seem confident, but my words came out miserable-sounding.

I was miserable. Liza had always been my best friend. I desperately didn't want to lose her, but I was shamed by her antics. I was miserable, too, because of the unkind way everyone treated Leeana. But mostly I was miserable because, in a dark corner of my heart, I thought she was right.

Chapter
10

❖

BACK IN THE SCHOOLHOUSE, Liza scooted to the far end of our bench. She jabbed chalk against her slate so hard she broke two pieces, and she sighed with more noise than I reckoned to be entirely necessary. She was subtracting fractions, so I guess that made her huffy, but part of the drama was just Liza, playing her forgiveness game.

I could have rescued her from some of those fractions, but I just let her suffer. She probably wouldn't have let me help anyway, so I read my history lesson.

That old flower book must have been too hard for Leeana, because she was reading one of the new ones Miss Jensen had brought from San Francisco. Its title was *Little Women*. It sounded like a little girl's story to me, though I will admit it was pretty thick. She concentrated hard, but at the rate she skimmed through the pages, I feared she wasn't getting much out of the story.

"Angelena and Liza, will you please come here?"

Miss Jensen stood beside her desk with our class book of poems in her hand. Each of us had used that book many times, for we were expected to memorize Bible verses at church school and poetry at regular school. Liza sighed mightily as we scooted off our bench.

Miss Jensen handed the book to her. "Choose a poem together and you can help each other memorize it. You will be expected to recite next Monday morning."

Liza and I paged through the poetry book. We had already used up all of the really short rhymes. It looked as if we were stuck with the longer ones.

Liza pointed. "Here's one about love by Robert Burns. He's one of the greatest poets ever."

All I knew about Robert Burns was that he was a Scot and he once wrote a poem to a *louse*, for heaven's sake. I figured that for the McCutcheon clan, his being a Scot was plenty of reason to call him the "greatest poet ever."

I liked this poem well enough, though, and I thought its being about love suited Liza. She just naturally liked to think about love. I followed along in the book while Liza closed her eyes and repeated the first verse. She only had to peek a few times in order to keep her place.

"O my Luve's like a red, red rose
    That's newly sprung in June:
O my Luve is like the melodie
    That's sweetly played in tune."

When she spoke she purred her *u*'s and *r*'s the way her father did. It made the poem more beautiful to listen to than it was to read.

"The spelling's off," I complained.

Liza hadn't noticed, but she squinted fiercely at the page. "That's 'cause it isn't English. It's Scots."

I reckoned Miss Jensen had noticed our quarrel. She was always telling us to solve our differences and make peace. I think that's why she had us working on the poem together and it did help us forget our disagreement. There were three more verses to learn. Before I knew, the time had passed and Miss Jensen announced dismissal.

I went out with Liza. We talked a bit more about the party before she headed west, toward her family's farm.

Evangeline was at Leeana's side, chattering like a chickadee, so fast and about so many things at once that Leeana held up her hand, palm outward, and laughed aloud. The sound reminded me of tiny bells, light as a rainbow except solid. It raised an echo from Evangeline, and soon I was pulled in, too.

The best glue I know of for friendship is shared laughter. That laughter also erased the last of the musty feelings Liza had put on my heart.

We started down Main Street. Evangeline started to tell us a story about Sarah's dog, but her prattle was interrupted by a wrathy shout. Mrs. Wilson burst out of the bakery door, giving the general impression of a steam tractor traveling downhill. She grabbed Evangeline's arm and swung her around. It startled me so that I didn't have a chance to defend her, and I knew Evangeline didn't dare to defend herself. We were always warned to mind adults, no matter what.

Mrs. Wilson was a balloon of a woman. She heaved herself from place to place, all the while emitting a breathy sound, as if she were leaking air.

She bent over Evangeline and hissed, "What will your mother say when she hears about you consorting with heathens? No telling what filth you might pick up and then carry along into decent society. You ought to be ashamed."

She glared over at me where I stood beside Leeana. "Shame on you, too, Angelena. You must not care about your folks at all! Your dad don't need trouble any more than the next person, and he sure don't need you to be the cause of it."

She dropped Evangeline's arm as if she were shaking some dirty rag. Evangeline came to me walking stifflike, with her chin so firm I guessed she would rather be whipped than shed a visible tear. I wrapped my arms around her.

Mrs. Wilson's curls shook with each step as she stomped back to the shop. She turned to glare at us a final time, filling the bakery doorway like rising dough. Gus and Gunnar grinned through the window like fools. One of them pulled his eyes slanty in a repeat of his performance of the day before.

I didn't feel the remotest urge to laugh at his mean-ness, but I did worry about Leeana seeing him. A glance told me she wasn't seeing anything. She stood ghost-silent beside me and stared holes into the ground.

"Get along, now." Mrs. Wilson's voice was harsh. "From here on, you be decent white girls and stick with your own kind."

She gave us a view of her backside as she plowed into the bakery. I could not help being reminded of Pa's mean old mule. The window shook when she slammed the door.

Evangeline trembled in my arms. It was like the day before, when she had escaped the attentions of that bobcat, except I felt Mrs. Wilson had frightened her considerably more.

"I don't understand. What did she mean about caus-ing trouble for Pa?"

Leeana spoke in a voice so quiet I had to strain to hear. "She meant you'd better not be seen with me. She meant they will find a way to punish your family for dealing with dirty Chinese."

She spun away from us, walking so fast we were forced to rush to catch up. When we did, I wasn't sure we were welcome.

"We don't pay any mind to people like the Wilsons." I was out of breath and couldn't manage to sound as convinced as I wanted to. "You haven't done us any kind of harm. Why, if you hadn't been there yesterday,

Evangeline and I might have had to wrestle with that bobcat."

Leeana didn't appear to hear me.

"We owe you a debt of gratitude and Mama wouldn't want us to be ungrateful, no matter what Mrs. Wilson says."

I hoped to sound convincing, but inside I was scared. What could they do to Pa?

Evangeline had something better than words to offer Leeana. She trotted even with her and grasped her hand tightly. Leeana's shoulders lost some of their starch. She even managed a smile when her mother came out to greet us.

"You girls are hungry, now? I have new buns just out of the oven."

Leeana relaxed a little more and joined in the flurry that followed as we arranged ourselves around Mrs. Lee's table.

"This will make the day more sweet." Mrs. Lee offered a chunk of honeycomb, dripping golden sweetness onto a white and blue plate. I knew without asking that it was from China Joe.

As for how Mrs. Lee knew our day needed sweetening, I could only figure that she was like all mothers. She just knew.

Evangeline was talkative as a gray squirrel at nut harvest. Leeana listened quietly at first, but soon she was laughing at Evangeline and chattering, too, telling

Mrs. Lee about the fight in the school yard the day before and how Miss Jensen had looked when she broke it up.

I closed my eyes for a moment, sitting at the big table amid the good smells and laughter. It didn't feel so very different from my own home.

When Mrs. Lee bent to place another plate on the table, a gold chain slipped from the neck of her dress. A hanging pendant caught the light. It was so lovely I stared.

Springtime green, pale as a new leaf, two carved dragons twisted together, forming an oval knot. It was beautiful and odd at the same time, like the joss house. Mrs. Lee saw me gaping.

I was mortified. Mama hated for us kids to act nosy. I quickly looked away, but Mrs. Lee didn't seem to think I was being impolite. She tenderly rubbed the carving between her slender fingers.

"This was a special gift. An Li's father gave it to me when I was a bride. I wear it always, for health and luck." She hesitated. "And to remember him."

"Where is he now?" Evangeline's boldness made me gasp.

I hadn't told Evangeline of my speculations that Mrs. Lee's real husband was Gin Lin and she had been put aside to make room for a new wife. It didn't seem any more far-fetched than lots of other things the Celestials did, but it wasn't the kind of thing to discuss with a second-grader. Still, as long as she had asked the question, I was eager to hear the answer. But Mrs. Lee's smile drifted off her face and even Evangeline looked as if she maybe should have shut trap.

At last Leeana broke the silence with a whisper. "He and Mother's youngest brother were working on a blasting crew up at Golden. They set a charge, but it didn't go off. My uncle went to check it. My father went to help him."

She studied her clasped hands in her lap. Mrs. Lee stood behind Leeana with her right hand resting lightly on Leeana's shoulder. She squeezed gently and finished the story.

"The evil demons must have been attracted by our happiness. They set the blast off just as my husband and my brother reached the black powder." A small sound might have been a cry that couldn't get all the way out. "Uncle Shoon brought us here, to make a life away from the danger in the mines. We please the gods because we feed people rather than tearing at the earth."

Her other hand caressed the dragon ornament.

"It's as green as a lacewing," Evangeline said. "What is it made of?"

"Ah, this is jade. We call it the 'Stone of Heaven,' and to us it is even more precious than gold."

I had seen plenty of gold, but that was my first glimpse of jade. Sitting at Mrs. Lee's table, I felt obliged to agree. Jade was more beautiful and must be more precious.

Chapter 11

THAT NIGHT AFTER DINNER, Pa and Tom played cribbage at the table. Evangeline and I sat and watched them, and Mama rocked by the fire with her knitting.

"Liza can hardly wait for Sunday, Tom." I couldn't help a little teasing. "She wanted me to guarantee you're coming along."

Tom scowled his way through the counting, then added up his own hand. "Fifteen-two, fifteen-four, and the rest don't score." He chucked his cards on the deck and moved his marker four holes forward on the board.

"And Tom, Liza said Belle's coming. I thought you would certain-sure want to know that."

Firelight made it hard to tell if he was blushing. He shrugged with an extra lot of shoulder action. "Don't make no matter to me at all. I guess I'll go along to be sure nothing happens to you, though."

A swelling of pride went through me. Last summer Tom had been my friend and I missed him sorely when he started to act so grown-up. It made me glad that he remembered how we used to watch out for each other.

"I can take care of myself." He would know I didn't exactly mean it.

"You? You're such a dang fool you would dance with a rattlesnake and thank his rattles for the music." He leaned back in his chair with his elbows bent and his thumbs hooked in his belt. Tom's hair is golden, especially in lamplight, and the fire made his dark eyes broody. I got a little glimpse of what Liza found so pleasing.

Pa reached for his pipe. "I don't know if I cotton to both of you being gone all day. There's plenty of chores to do here, especially now that school has started. Your mama needs the help, and I could use a little more than I've been getting at the diggin's."

"I'll help," Evangeline said, calm as you please. "Angelena doesn't get to go very often. I'll mind the baby and say *double* prayers."

"Angelena will say her own prayers," Mama said. "But I allow you're big enough to handle little Reuben."

She turned to Pa. "You won't be working on the Sabbath, anyway, and the children need some recreation. They could benefit from a day of entertainment with their friends."

"They aren't so all-fired friendly." Evangeline tossed her head and made her braids dance. "They wouldn't hardly speak to us at school, and Liza was huffy as a wet cat."

"Liza got a little perturbed, is all, but she did enjoy the rolls you sent, Mama." I truly hoped to change the topic. Evangeline would not cooperate.

"Mrs. Wilson made an awful fuss. She said we'd bring harm on the whole family. Besides, she hurt my arm something dreadful."

I was aware of stretched-out quiet. Mama's needles and rocker stopped. The sound of Pa pulling air into his pipe was the only thing between us and total silence.

When Pa spoke, it was in a faraway, thoughtful tone. "Did she say what kind of harm?"

"No, just that we were consorting with heathens and we would bring bad things home with us. She said we would be sorry if we didn't stop." She settled little Reuben on her lap. "Pa, what does it mean, to 'consort with heathens'?"

"It means nonsense, that's what it means." Tom's voice was rough-edged. "Why would anyone say such a thing about you, anyway? You aren't keeping company with any dang Celestials, are you?"

"No, only with Leeana and Mrs. Lee."

Evangeline didn't notice Tom's surprise. She went on with her tale, thinking as little as usual and talking as fast as she could.

"Oh, Mama, their church is so beautiful! It has crooked paths and high doors to keep the demons out and fire-protection dragons on the top. The worshipers make music, sort of like the Catholics, only with drums and gongs instead of bells. Their church smells of incense, like the Catholics, too. The Catholics aren't heathens, are they, Mama?"

Mama contemplated Evangeline with a look of astonishment, then she slowly shook her head. "No, honey, their form of worship is a little different, but they worship the same God we do." She turned a grave look on Tom and added, "Remember, that same God told us to love one another. You don't need to follow Jasper in every folly, Tom. I know you admire him, but you're old enough to think for yourself."

I wasn't used to Mama being so direct with Tom and I sure wasn't used to hearing her speak ill of Jasper, even in such a mild way. Tom might have been a bit surprised, too, for he was silent. I was right relieved that Evangeline stayed silent, too, especially about the nature and number of those demons.

Mama bent to take the baby from her and said, "Now show me your arm. You say Mrs. Wilson hurt you and I want to see."

She satisfied herself that Evangeline wasn't bruised and announced that it was time for bed. Later, as I basked in Evangeline's warmth, I practiced my poem.

"O, my luve is like a red, red rose." I whispered into the dark, trying to purr the *r*'s and *u*'s the way Liza had done. I fell asleep listening to Evangeline's breathing and rain pouring from the sky onto our roof.

The rain kept up through the next two days. By the end of school on Friday, Liza was plumb discouraged. She stood on the schoolhouse porch and wrapped Miss

Jensen's poetry book in oilskin, for she wanted to practice the Scot's poem in front of her parents. She gazed at the sky.

"It looks like gray pudding." She wrinkled her nose when George Gustafson dashed by, splashing water onto our feet. "This weather is going to ruin everything. Even if it clears, it's too damp to keep a person's hair from frizzing. I expect we won't see another ray of sunshine until spring."

Chapter 12

THE RAINS LASTED through Saturday, but Liza must have been saying extra prayers for good weather, for Sunday morning dawned fair and bright.

Mama helped me pack a picnic lunch big enough for sharing. She combed my hair with a part down the middle as straight as a piece of string.

"Shall I wind it into a coil for you?" She spoke around a mouthful of hairpins.

"No, Mama. I'll be bouncing on Turnip all day and it'll just shake loose. Better to start with it hanging down, since it'll certain-sure end that way."

She placed the hairpins in her dresser box, then put her cool hand against my cheek and gave me a love gaze. "You're so nearly grown, Angelena. I do prefer you with your hair down, like a girl. No need for you to grow up too fast."

I knew what she meant. I felt the same way, wanting one moment to be a proper lady and the next to be as carefree as Evangeline. I had seen Jasper turn earnest, and Tom seemed to be catching some of it, too. I guessed I would have plenty of time for serious matters when I was finished with school and ready to wed. I promised myself to squander this day on fun.

Mama tied a blue ribbon in my hair and left it to cascade down my back. The locks did curl some, and she encouraged them with a curling iron warmed on the stove. I wore my best blue calico dress, which meant I would have to ride lady-style.

Mama let me wear her blue sweater against the autumn chill. Blue is my best color, and my favorite. My heart was full of expectation as I set forth into the blue-sky day.

Tom whistled while he cinched up the horses' saddles. He was to ride his favorite mount, Majesty; I chose Turnip, our gentle mare.

Charlie greeted us when we got to the Gustafsons', but we had to wait on Tony. He was still a bit sleep-rumpled when he mounted Daisy, but his big smile was square on his face as usual.

It being Sunday, the bakery was closed. Liza, Gunnar, and Gus waited out front with Liza's older sister, Belle. I allow Tom brightened when he saw her.

Greetings were exchanged all around. Liza was lively with her smiles and aimed a good portion of them at Tom, though I'm not convinced he gave them special notice.

She did look peart! Her big-brimmed bonnet was a

shade of green that reminded me of Mrs. Lee's jade pendant. It framed her face and set off her burnished gold hair. It was a practical choice as well, for it kept the sun's glare off her face and reduced her squinting considerably.

Tony and the Wilson twins said hello to each other civil-like but I noticed they rode far apart when we started through China Shacks. In spite of the Sabbath, the washhouse was open and smoke rose from the stovepipe. Sam Wise sat in the doorway of his store, having a quick-paced discussion with two men. It might have seemed like an argument to my friends, but I guessed it was conversation. China Shacks was less of a cipher to me, now that I had walked through it a time or two.

Hands raised in greeting from a cluster of old men, and one called out, "Hello, First Angel." I said, "Hello," ignoring Liza's look of scorn. Except I couldn't ignore the way Gus Wilson directed his horse right toward them, and forced them aside. I knew it was Gus because his horse was a roan. Gunnar rode a dappled mare.

Tom didn't notice any of this. He was entirely occupied in riding close to Belle.

Leeana's door was closed. The curtains were drawn, but I thought I saw a flutter of movement there. Mrs. Lee must have taken a day of rest, for there was no smoke rising from her chimney, and Buttermilk stood in the field.

The road wound beside Bunkum Creek, north toward the Rogue River. Sometimes the trail dwindled and we had to pick our way through vast areas blighted by diggin's. I was shocked to realize how much of the creekside had been washed plumb away.

Once the gravels near the creek were exhausted, the miners began to work the terraces above the streambed, and that tore up the land something fierce. Whole hills were washed downstream, leaving gaping holes, with here and there an "island" of earth that showed how far above us the surface used to be. The countryside looked like a mouthful of bad teeth.

I murmured "Whoa" to Turnip at the edge of Poorman's Flat. A group of Chinese miners were fixing to get their hydraulic giant into operation.

Liza stopped beside me, giggling at something Gus had whispered. She was paying extra-close attention to Gus and Gunnar, but I saw her steal glances at Tom now and then, too. Tom's glances stayed close attached to Belle.

Tony rode up beside me, already talking before he had rightly arrived. "There's miles of ditches up on top of these hills, just waiting for a rain. With the drenching we've had this week, there'll be plenty of water for hydraulicking."

Tony can manage to act excited and dreamy at the same time. I recognized the attitude and settled back for a listen.

"It's called 'scientific mining' because it uses gravity."

He pointed to a huge wood box perched up on the hill. "That's the head box. The water goes through there and down those pipes. By the time it gets to creek level, it's moving right powerful. They just send it along canvas hoses to the giant."

The "giant" was a huge brass nozzle. I reckoned it was rightly named, for the operator was Chinese, and small like most Celestials, but this nozzle was every inch as tall as he was. He grasped a set of handles on each side of the giant in a way that made me think of a drover trying to hold back a whole team of mules. He was aided by a counterbalance, a bucket full of rock that hung off the back of the contraption.

"A really good giant operator can carve up a hill like a leg of lamb." Tony still looked dreamy. I guessed he was using his imagination to whittle some gold out of that hill.

"I saw one of those fellows knock a Canada goose right out of the sky," Tom said as he reined up Majesty. "I reckon they had a celebration feast that night."

Belle gasped and looked at Tom with wide eyes. "Imagine that. Right out of the sky. Do you suppose those Celestials cooked it first?"

"Depends on how hungry they were, I guess. I hear tell they eat almost anything, cooked or not. Even maggots and rats."

Belle shuddered prettily and shied back a little from the scene in front of us, but I felt interested in the goings-on. I edged Turnip forward so I could watch.

Brass gleamed in the sunlight. The Celestial grasped the giant's handles and spread his legs wide, then shouted something in Chinese. A second man bent over a huge wheel-valve that was over a foot across and strained to turn it. The valve squealed. Water commenced to flow, then to erupt from the giant in a mighty torrent.

The Celestial leaned back as the force increased. He turned slowly to aim the stream and swept it in a huge arc. Water sliced the earth, carrying the side of the hill down and away toward Bunkum Creek.

Sluice boxes, like wood troughs, had been placed in the water's path. Riffles across their bottoms caught the heavy gold and let the water go along its journey to the creek, then the Rogue River, and finally, I hear say, to the deep ocean.

The gold stayed put, mixed with gravel on the floor of the sluice boxes. In the cleanup, all that gold and gravel would be washed again. Pure gold would be separated out and gravel tailings piled off to the side. When I looked more closely, I realized that our horses were actually standing on tailings from previous years.

Humans alone could never have made a profit just by digging in the high terraces above the river. It would take too much time and toil. But the cleverness of the miners, combined with the considerable strength of flowing water, gleaned the earth's treasure.

"That's the smartest way to work a claim," Tony said as we watched the man aim and cut with his water knife. The sound of water and rustling gravel blended with miners' urgent shouts, as they used shovels to keep the water's path clear and crowbars to move rolling boulders aside.

"They weren't miners back in China, you know. They were farmers. But they understand how to irrigate fields, and it isn't so different, really. It's all about managing water, whether you plant crops or harvest gold."

Charlie had been patient with us while we watched, but now he was anxious to get to Golden, and his girl. He urged his horse forward through the tumult, and we followed. Old Turnip carried me gently, in spite of the uncertain footing offered by the rocky edge of Bunkum Creek. I think she was relieved to get away from the noise, and I was glad to get on with our adventure, too.

A lone rider stood beside the trail ahead. At first I didn't recognize Jasper, for his hat was pulled low and he had a neckerchief that 'most covered his chin. He greeted us friendly enough, though.

"I thought I'd ride along. Be sure you don't get attacked by heathens or suchlike."

Tony snorted behind me, but both Belle and Liza seemed eager for Jasper's offer of protection. I noticed Tom kept Majesty between Belle and Jasper.

Chapter
13
❖

WE PASSED four more groups of men working hard, and half a dozen claims had the look of being long abandoned. At one busy diggin's a group of Celestials leaned on their shovels and waved at us.

"Greedy heathens," Gus Wilson muttered. "They work any day of the week. They don't understand the meaning of a Sabbath."

"They're taking advantage of the rains. I saw some white men working at the last place," Tony said. "Are they heathens, too?"

Gunnar came to his brother's defense. "The reason they have to work on Sunday is that the dang Celestials are threatening to carry off all the gold. They won't be satisfied until they've robbed every last speck and sent it back to China."

Jasper chimed in. "You've figured that out just right. They work for themselves and keep to themselves, and never give a nickel or a thought about what's good for

America." He leaned toward Tom to address him directly. "Isn't that right, Tom?"

"I reckon so," Tom said. "They do have that habit of going back to China, alive or dead." He shuddered, probably remembering those "disgustin'" jars of bones.

I felt the need of a new subject for conversation. "Here's the river, at last."

Where Bunkum Creek flows into the Rogue, the water is swift and swirly. The riverbed is filled with huge boulders and is not good for mining.

A great blue heron waded in the shallows with a haughty gait that reminded me of Mrs. Wilson when she wore her dignity and wasn't mad. A kingfisher swooped low over the water but landed on a branch with his bill empty.

"Just showing off," Tom said, and Belle rewarded his cleverness with a bright smile.

About half a mile upriver, the Rogue parted to flow on each side of a patch of high ground we called Deer Island. Deer liked to browse there and they had no trouble in reaching the brush-covered island, for the river flowed slow and shallow between it and the shore. At the forest edge stood a plank shack, and around the shack were scattered about half a dozen beehives.

I recognized China Joe hunkered at the water's edge. He was pulling up moss and grass and piling it on a piece of canvas. A big wood box stood nearby, with a rounded bottom and handles sticking out from each end.

The work was easier with two, but one man could operate a rocker if need be, sloshing the grass and water back and forth inside the box until gold sank out of the roots and sand. If it were a lucky day, a nugget might be left behind as well. Grass mining wouldn't make anybody rich, but it could keep a person fed. He looked up at the sound of our passing and waved with some enthusiasm. I waved back, as I had to Sam Wise, knowing I would have to tolerate sneers from Liza.

She hadn't even noticed, for she was talking to Tom, but Jasper did and he took exception. "Watch your manners, Angelena. You have no call to embarrass us with your foolishness."

I had been taught to mind my elders, but Jasper was only seven years older than I was in age, and sometimes I considered him to be seven years younger in behavior. Still, he was family, and I did not want to cause a ruckus in front of the others.

"He isn't doing harm," I muttered. "He's only grass mining. He earns his keep with honeybees."

Jasper scowled, then looked up at the hives with his eyes slitted down. Without a word, he wheeled his horse and dropped back to the rear. He continued the ride beside Gus, and I was glad for his absence. The straight-up truth is, Turnip was better company than Jasper.

We marked our trail with laughter. The morning had slipped away before Charlie gave a mighty whoop and galloped around a bend, covering the last hundred yards to the stage station at Golden in extra-fast time.

A pretty girl light-footed out of the building and into the autumn sunshine. She smiled a greeting to us all, but mostly it fastened on Charlie. Tess had rosy cheeks and hair the color of a horse chestnut. In moments we were clustered together, undergoing introductions all around.

The Sunday stage from San Francisco was expected, but Tess's mother waved us on. "You young folks go have fun. We can handle any kind of crowd the stage will bring."

She looked to me like it was so, too, for she had a wide stance and muscular arms. She carried a long mixing spoon in one hand and her hair was covered with a calico bandana. Temptatious smells wafted out of the stagehouse kitchen, and I almost envied those dusty travelers who would be having Sunday supper there.

Tess helped Charlie load a canvas bag onto her mare. From the good smells surrounding that bag, I guessed we were going to have something of a Sunday supper, too. Charlie helped her mount, looking more gallant than I had ever seen him. Courting helps a person's manners something fierce.

Just as we left, the San Francisco stage pulled in. Inside were two men, who alighted as soon as the stagecoach came to a full stop, and bustled into the stagehouse. On the outside rode three Celestials. They climbed down, quietlike, and settled on the edge of the porch to eat. Their dark clothes and faces were covered with dust.

It was such a happy day for me I guess I wanted the joy to be more complete. I braved myself up a little to say out loud, "It seems they'd get less dusty if they rode inside the coach."

Tess's eyes widened at the thought.

"Dear me, no," she said. "Chinamen always ride on top. It wouldn't do to put them inside with the regular folks. Why, that would be a perfect laugh!"

She gave a perfect laugh then, directed mostly at Charlie. They rode off side by side and the rest of us followed. This time I tagged along at the end of the line. Tony stayed with me.

He noticed that I was bothered. "Don't worry, Angelena. This is a good day to be out in the fresh air."

"But they'd be riding outside even if it were raining, wouldn't they?" It wasn't really a question.

"I expect so." It wasn't really an answer.

I knew I couldn't change the way the coach lines operated. The men had been dusty, but after all, they didn't seem unhappy. I admit I soon forgot them in our fun.

The picnic party was grand. We ate and teased and played a game of charades. Charlie Gustafson played his harmonica and we all sang. At the end, he played "Lorena," a song of love and longing. He gazed at Tess while he played and she gazed right back at him. He was wise to bring his harmonica, for I have heard Charlie sing with his natural voice.

Too soon, we had to return to the station and leave off Tess. We were a merry party on the way home. Jasper led the entertainment, playacting Charlie's antics, now that his lady was not present to see. We all teased him mightily and he teased us back, pointing out that Tom and Belle had made a team all day. Liza's eyes went all squinty at that.

She rode far ahead with Jasper and the Wilson twins. Their conversation was lively at first, then dropped into a muffled tone that made me think they were discussing secrets again, but this time I didn't let them concern me. Charlie, Tom, and Belle chatted together in an amiable way, and that left me in company with Tony.

Tony and his younger brother were a combination at the school, but when Tony was on his own, he acted about as polite as any boy could. He rode easy on Daisy and told me of his plans. I was starting to get used to that dreamy look. "I figure fruit trees could make a man a living in this country after the gold is panned out. That won't be so long, either. The first miners have taken whatever they could get easy. With the Chinese cleaning out the tailings, that will be the end of it." He was silent for a while, then added, "Grapes would make a good crop, too."

Neither Daisy nor Turnip was anxious to make speed, so we had fallen farther behind the others. A mighty commotion suddenly erupted ahead of us. Shouts and gunshots rang through the autumn air.

"Stay here," Tony shouted and urged Daisy forward. Of course I hurried after him.

We rounded a sharp bend in the river in time to see the Wilson boys shooting skyward and dashing their horses back and forth between China Joe's cabin and the river. China Joe was alone on the rocky shore. His eyes were huge and his hands in the air with fingers spread wide. His hat had fallen off and his pigtail bounced. His bare feet jittered over the rocks as he half-ran and half-danced toward the water.

Tony hollered and rode hard. "Come on," he shouted to Tom and Charlie as he galloped by. They followed, but at a slower pace.

Jasper and the Wilson boys heard Tony's fuss. They holstered their guns and trotted back to the main trail, where Liza waited. They were laughing, and so was Liza. Charlie and Tony looked disgusted and Belle's eyes were wide with shock, and maybe fear.

I searched Tom's face and found him serious-quiet. There was no laughter in him, but he hadn't tried to stop the ruckus, either. He turned away from me to escort Belle along the trail home.

As we rode, I stole a single glance back at China Joe. He stood stiffly at the river's edge, staring after us. He had picked up his hat and held it before his chest like a shield.

Chapter 14

THE AUTUMN WEATHER had granted one beautiful day for our party. On Monday morning, the rain came back. The log across Bunkum Creek was slippery-wet. Still, it was broad enough to cross in safety. Evangeline and I took extra care.

Buttermilk stood, head down, under his plank rain shelter. Leeana waited on the porch, wrapped in a stained slicker. She held a little oilskin-wrapped bundle. On her feet were miner's gum boots, which would surely keep her dry but put her in some danger of tripping and breaking her neck, for they were overlarge. I expected she had her cloth shoes on inside those boots, with plenty of room left over.

Through the window I could see Mrs. Lee and Uncle Shoon filling baskets with freshly baked buns. They called out greetings, but they were too busy to stop and chat. I was sorry, for I wasn't anxious to confront the reserve in Leeana's eyes.

I decided the best thing was to explain right out about the party. "Charlie Gustafson is sweet on a girl up at Golden. Her name is Tess. Er . . . well, her folks run the stage station."

Leeana listened, but didn't contribute any conversation. I went on, too fast. "There was a picnic party yesterday. A bunch of us rode up."

I thought a "bunch of us" was close enough. No need to point out that the whole population of Bounty between the ages of fourteen and twenty-three had been invited, except for Leeana.

She tucked the packet under her slicker.

"Not everyone went. Evangeline had to stay home and do chores. It was just a few of us, really."

"I know. I watched you ride by." She stepped off the porch into the muddy street. "Come on. We'll be late."

It was a relief to duck my head against the rain and slosh up Main Street. We rushed, so there was no extra breath for conversation. When we got to school, Leeana carried her bundle directly to Miss Jensen.

Evangeline and I shrugged off our wet coats and huddled close to the wood stove. Tony Gustafson had come early to help build the fire. The heavy stove door creaked when he opened it to add wood. There was a satisfying bang when he shut it and stepped back, so the wetter newcomers could gather close. The smell of hot, wet wool spread through the room.

looked anxiously for Liza. She had the poetry book, and I wished for her to test my memory before our recitation. We would have to be hasty, for the recitation began first thing. At the last minute before the bell, Liza dashed in. She was in company with the Wilson boys and they barely had time to reach their seats before the first bell rang.

"Do you know the poem?" she hissed.

"I hope so. I thought we were going to practice before school."

"Belle got me up too late. I didn't have time to learn it."

She huddled over the poetry book, so close I couldn't see past her blonde curls to the page. Her lips moved silently. I had no chance at all to check my recollection before Miss Jensen called for attention.

Recitations always started with the lower grades. Sarah stood facing us in front of the blackboard. She grinned widely, and I saw she had a new space where a tooth had gone missing. We all laughed at that, but I don't think Sarah knew why we laughed, or cared. She was used to causing people amusement, and I do think she enjoyed it.

Her recitation was a short poem about a boy chasing a pig and winding up—*SPLAT*—in the mud. When Sarah got to the splat part, she clapped her hands together smartly and shouted out the word. That earned her more laughter.

Evangeline did a very pretty recitation about a bird with a yellow bill. She shook her pigtails vigorously when she got to the last line, "Ain't you shamed, you sleepyhead?"

Miss Jensen gently explained the proper word was "aren't," but Evangeline sat down so fast I wasn't absolute-sure she heard.

Liza peered at the poetry book and tapped her toe in rhythm with the Robert Burns poem. I was nervous, too, but she still held the book so close I couldn't peek at it.

At last it was our turn. We went up together and stood side by side. After a bit of jostling, it was determined that I should go first.

I tried not to look at Gus and Gunnar, who were stiff and properlike whenever Miss Jensen faced their way. When she turned to me and Liza, though, they crossed their eyes and wiped their brows, as if to say they expected to be pained by our performance. I looked at Tony, instead. At least he wasn't making faces at us, although I suspected he was more concerned with his fire than with our poetry.

I got through the poem, stumbling over the way I should pronounce "luve" and settling on plain "love." I finished all four verses with only a few small stumbles and an enormous amount of relief.

Miss Jensen made a mark in her grading book and said, "Thank you, Angelena. The only thing I can suggest to improve your recitation is that you should look more directly at your audience. It will help your expression, and it will help keep their interest."

"Yes, ma'am," I said. That was what you were always supposed to say.

"Liza?" Miss Jensen provided an encouraging smile.

Liza gave her head a little shake and took a step forward. She opened her mouth to say the poem, but not a word came out. She cleared her throat and tried again.

"My luve is like a red, red rose
That's sweetly played in tune.
My luve is like a melody
That's newly sprung in June."

She seemed to realize that she had left out two words, because she blurted, "Oh!" and then repeated, "Oh!" Then she was silent. Evidently the next verse evaded her.

Miss Jensen frowned and made a mark in her book. "Liza, perhaps you could do the poem again for us next week. You have all the words in verse one, but they aren't all in the correct order."

I heard a whoof of muffled laughter from the rear of the room, but couldn't tell which twin it came from. Liza blushed scarlet, but she managed a "Yes, ma'am" before she led the way back to our seat. I hoped she didn't see Gus and Gunnar making moony faces and rolling their eyes at our mushy love poem.

"Class, we have a special treat today." Miss Jensen beamed in the direction of our bench, and Leeana stirred beside me. "Leeana has brought a book of Chinese poetry. I had an opportunity to learn about this exquisite form of literature when I was at the Normal School in San Francisco, and I'm glad for you to have a chance to hear it, too. Leeana has offered to recite the poem in Chinese and then to translate it for us. Leeana?"

She slid off the bench and walked up to the front with the tiny steps that were her version of company manners. In her hand was a little book bound in red silky stuff and decorated with gold embroidery. Bowing slightly, she opened the book.

At first I was afraid she was going to make an entire fool of herself, for she opened it from the wrong end, but she found her place well enough and spoke in a clear voice.

The Chinese I heard spoken on the street sounded boisterous to me, like the sound of rocks bouncing through a sluice box. But when Leeana read her poem, her voice was soft, like water stirring pebbles.

I glanced at Liza, but she was sitting with her arms crossed high across her chest, her eyes narrow slits and her chin all jutted out. I didn't think she was feeling at all charitable toward Leeana. Perhaps she wasn't paying any attention at all. She might have been too wrathy about her own performance to notice anyone else.

When the little poem was finished, Leeana bowed to us and took a deep breath. "This is what the poem says in English:

Jade-colored beetles crawl
Among petals of gold chrysanthemum.
No danger here,
For jade can't tarnish gold."

The class responded with silence. She nodded deeply, once, and returned to sit beside me. I winked congratulations, but Liza stayed stiff-necked and stared forward. Miss Jensen wrote in her book, and thanked Leeana, then gave us all a lecture on different languages and poetry styles.

We were forced to eat lunch at our seats, for the rain continued ferocious. Liza was chatty and enthusiastic to a suspicious degree. She raised her chin and looked past her nose toward Leeana, using an exaggerated tone that almost sounded like Miss Jensen.

"That was an interesting poem you read. Of course, in this school, we are expected to do memory work, but I'm sure that with extra help you will catch on to that."

It sounded more like criticism than generosity to me. I can't say how Leeana took it. She whispered, "Thank you," and ate very slowly, with tiny bites that made her always seem to be chewing, with no room for talking.

Liza went on. "It's the same with reading. Proper English is very difficult. If you start slowly, you should be able to find a suitable book. I'm sure some of the lower grades have something at your level."

Liza tossed her head in a proud sweep and smiled all around. She was a picture of a gracious lady being kind to someone who needed kindness, but might not really have earned it. I had a surprise for her.

While Leeana had read from her Chinese book, a thought had come to me. I should have realized it before, except I so expected a Chinese girl to be ignorant of English reading. Finally, I understood why Miss Jensen kept giving Leeana different books.

"Liza," I said, "Leeana isn't having trouble with English. She finishes a book every few days. Miss Jensen can't keep up with her."

I admit to some satisfaction at seeing Liza's haughty expression freeze. Her eyes and lips formed narrow lines and her cheeks brightened considerably. She snorted.

"Reading doesn't make proper Americans. She's a heathen and she'll never truly understand American ways. There's no help for it."

I honestly felt puzzled. "Liza, what are American ways anyway? I used to think America was about lots of kinds of folks being free together. Now I'm not so sure."

Leeana didn't comment, but her manner toward me was more relaxed as we walked through town after school. I guess I had partly redeemed myself for the awkwardness about our picnic party.

Her mother greeted us with a new treat, a kind of boiled dumpling filled with sweet plum jam. Evangeline ate two and murmured in appreciation. I ate one. Only good manners kept me from having another.

We had said, "Thank you," and were starting to say good-bye when a hollow thump sounded on the porch, followed by pounding that shook the door.

Leeana's mother tensed. Her hand moved to her throat and clutched the jade dragons. Her eyes made me think of a deer's at the sound of gunfire. Leeana jumped up, knocking her chair over, and took a step toward the door. Mrs. Lee stopped her with a frantic gesture.

She edged up to the window and eased aside the curtain, then spoke in rapid Chinese.

Leeana released the door latch. Uncle Shoon must have been leaning against it, for it swung open with the weight of his body. He slumped across the threshold. Red, red blood made a stark contrast with his snowy hair.

Chapter 15

❖

MRS. LEE KNELT beside her uncle, holding his head. Evangeline fetched a bowl of water and Leeana gathered a bundle of the wrapping cloths to clean and bind his wound. We found a quilt to cover him, for he was shivering mightily.

Leeana and her mother spoke together in Chinese, then Leeana rushed out the door. Evangeline and I stayed to help Mrs. Lee. Quick footsteps on the porch, then Sam Wise burst in with Leeana close behind.

Uncle Shoon being a small man and not too heavy a burden, we soon had him on Mrs. Lee's bed, and wrapped him in more warm quilts. Sam Wise bent his head and, with eyes closed, ran his fingers lightly along Uncle Shoon's wrists. Leeana and her mother watched in respectful silence.

"What's he doing?" Evangeline whispered.

"Pulses." Leeana whispered, too. "Sam Wise is a famous pulsologist. He can tell how serious Uncle's injuries are just by touching his wrists."

Evidently there was some reason for optimism there, for soon Uncle Shoon was propped up by pillows, sipping tea from a little bowl-shaped cup that he cradled in his palms like a warming flame.

He spoke quietly with Sam Wise, their heads bent close. I couldn't understand their words, but something they said made Leeana stiffen. Her eyes went from anxious to angry. Mrs. Lee wiped her forehead with the back of her arm and turned away with a soft cry.

It was clear that we were no longer useful. Indeed, we were in the way.

"It's past time for us to be home," I said, and I was grateful when Evangeline didn't object.

We got home out of breath from our dash up the hill. We truly were late. I wanted to tell Mama about the excitement, but she had no time for conversation. She was busy, with steaming pots on the stove and Reuben crying in her arms.

She frowned us into action. Molly must be milked, the pigs and chickens fed, eggs gathered, and the table set. The baby needed minding, and the wood box needed filling, and then there was dinner to cook, and eat, and clean away. Most times Tom helped with some of that, especially the eating, but that night neither he nor Jasper came home for our evening meal.

That nettled Mama some, too. "At least they could tell me before I cook for them." She surveyed their two empty places.

"More for the rest of us." Pa smiled and reached for a second helping of squash. I wasn't sure he was really that hungry, but he made Mama smile, too.

We had nearly finished eating when Tom came in, closing the door softly and murmuring answers to Mama's questions.

"Jasper had some people he wanted to see. I just tagged along, is all. Then I stopped to visit Charlie Gustafson at his claim. It took longer than I planned."

He didn't look Mama straight on, but ducked his head and muttered. He said he wasn't very hungry and he was mighty sorry to be late. He did agree to a helping of venison stew and some apple cobbler.

While he was eating, Jasper came in. His face was red from cold and he thumped his feet on the floor in front of the stove.

"Been riding hard," he explained to Mama's questioning glance. "Had to see some folks on the other side of town."

He didn't explain any more, but he did take two helpings of stew. Right after he ate, he excused himself and was gone.

"What's rushing him?" Pa regarded the closed door with some wonder. "He couldn't be bothered much with work this afternoon, either. You'd think he was a man of some importance, considering the flurry he's always in."

It occurred to me that Jasper might be right familiar with the insides of the gambling saloon, but I didn't offer my opinion. It didn't do to be too involved when Mama and Pa discussed her little brother.

Mama let the matter lie, and Pa appeared satisfied that he had said enough. Soon the house was peaceful. We settled around the fire.

Tom and Pa sat at the table with the cribbage board between them. Tom shuffled the cards with the deep *brrrrrp* sound of a practiced card player, then offered the deck to Pa. He rapped the top with a knuckle to tell Tom he should go ahead and deal. It was a familiar ritual, and it helped me push aside worrisome thoughts of Uncle Shoon.

Evangeline sat on a low stool. Her tongue stuck out from between her teeth and she breathed noisily, as she concentrated on her knitting. She was working on her first project, a little sweater for her doll.

I sat on our warm braided rug with the baby snuggled beside me. Mama settled into her rocker, picked up one of Evangeline's knee-high stockings, and patiently started to darn the heel. I worked on a pair of winter socks for Tom.

"I suppose Uncle Shoon just fell off Buttermilk." Evangeline's eyes never left her knitting.

"Why do you say that?" Mama's rocker slowed, then stopped.

"He came home with his head cut. It was awful. Mrs. Lee was really upset."

"Angelena? What does she mean?" Mama's eyes targeted me.

"We walked Leeana home and Mrs. Lee invited us in. Uncle Shoon delivers her special buns up to the diggin's. He got hurt somehow." I held my breath and hoped I had explained enough to satisfy Mama without causing her concern.

"His head was all bloody and he bled on the floor, too," Evangeline said. "Mrs. Lee sent for the doctor."

"Doctor Hanks is up at Tiller," Mama said. "That's a long way to go."

"Oh, no. She sent for Doctor Wise." Evangeline's voice was confident. "He's a pulsologist, and he's a friend of Uncle Shoon. He came right away."

"What's that?" Pa folded his cards and put them facedown on the table. "Why did they need a doctor?"

Tom didn't look up from his cards. He studied them hard and rearranged them twice.

When I had explained again, Pa turned to Tom. "Do you know anything about this?"

"No, Pa. I told you. I saw some folks with Jasper, then I rode over to the Gustafsons' claim. I was with Charlie."

"I didn't ask, 'Did you do it?' I asked if you know anything about it."

Pa's voice was as stern as I've ever heard it, and I know Tom noticed, for he firmed up his jaw and swallowed before he answered.

"No, Pa. Some of the guys were talking about the Celestials and how they should go back to China. I just listened for a while and then I went to see Charlie."

"Where did Jasper go?"

Mama gasped. "R. C., you hadn't better accuse Jasper without reason."

"I know, Bertie. I'm not accusing. But Jasper talks mighty big, and I can't be blamed for thinking."

"Do your thinking away from our girls. Life can seem ugly enough without us making it harder for them."

Pa grunted around his pipe. He picked up his cards and sighed, then muttered, "I suppose that burro might have slipped him off."

They played out the hand, and it was Pa's turn to shuffle. Tom studied the cribbage board as if he could learn his future there. Mama picked up her darning and recommended rocking.

I let my breathing go back to normal, but Pa had given me plenty to think about.

Chapter
16

❖

"YOU TAKE THESE APPLES along to Mrs. Lee." Mama held out a basket brimming with just-picked fruit. "And you tell her I'm sorry for her troubles."

She dipped a rag in water and wrapped it gently around the stems of a bunch of Gloriosa daisies. Then she tucked them into the basket. Their rust-and-gold blossoms made a picture against the ruby-red apples.

I gave Mama an extra-long hug. Evangeline fairly skipped out the door with the basket over her arm. I caught up with her halfway down the hill.

The aroma of fresh buns welcomed us as usual, but Mrs. Lee's curtains were drawn tight shut. The sound of my knocking echoed extra loud in all the quiet.

Leeana peered out at us. "Come in," she whispered.

"How is your uncle Shoon?" I whispered, too.

"He can talk with us, but he gets dizzy if he sits up. Sam Wise says he must stay in bed a little longer."

Mrs. Lee bent over the stove with her shoulders

hunched into a protective curve. She nodded to us, but didn't say anything.

Evangeline offered the basket. "Our mama sent these for you. She said she's sorry for all your troubles." Even in faint light, the fruit and flowers seemed to glow, red and gold as a sunset.

It was as if someone lighted a candle behind Mrs. Lee's face. She took the basket from Evangeline and thanked her with a dignified bow.

"To put red and gold together means happiness and good luck. Please tell your mother 'Thank you.'" She gave the basket to Leeana. "Show your uncle how kind Mrs. Stuart has been to us."

Leeana padded back to the bedroom in her quiet cloth shoes. I heard conversation with that peculiar Chinese lilt, then she came out, closing the door gently. "He says to please thank your mother. He says she makes him feel much better with her good wishes."

A footstep sounded on the porch, followed by a knock. The door opened a crack. China Joe's face appeared, then he nudged the door wider and came in. He had a jar of golden honey in his right hand. In his left, he carried a book. He handed the book to Leeana, nodded to Mrs. Lee, and muttered, "Hello, Angels," to us, but he didn't linger. He carried the honey directly into the bedroom.

I knew he must be anxious to see Uncle Shoon, but I also thought he might be ashamed, remembering the way I had seen him dance to the tune of Gus Wilson's gun. I hadn't been able to look at him straight on. Somehow, I felt ashamed, too.

"We'd better go." I yearned for fresh air and sunlight.

I was glad to reach the schoolhouse steps. Miss Jensen waited there with cheerful words and a welcoming smile. She was extra kind to Leeana and acted right pleased to receive the book Leeana handed her. It was the one China Joe had brought.

The day progressed as usual, with lessons and lunch, mischief and merriment. Now and then, the sky turned particularly dark and rain splattered the windows. We were obliged to eat inside again, but Leeana didn't have to tolerate Liza's elegant disdain. She and Miss Jensen worked together at the sand table.

At first I was glad that Leeana was getting practice writing English. Then I realized that I had misunderstood Leeana once again.

Mama had put a considerable piece of cake in my lunch. It seemed she must have meant for me to share it. I gave some to Liza and took a portion to Evangeline in the second-grade row.

I hadn't intended to be nosy, but it was necessary for me to walk close by the sand table. Miss Jensen had propped China Joe's book open on the windowsill. Leeana was drawing in the sand, but I saw she was not practicing cursive. She was making Chinese characters like the ones in China Joe's book. Miss Jensen carefully copied each one. Leeana was teaching Miss Jensen Chinese writing!

I neglected to explain what Leeana was doing when I sat down again next to Liza. She would either not like what I said or not believe it. It was safer to talk about dresses, hairstyles, and boys, or rather to listen. One of the things I admired about Liza was that she was social as the center pup. She was comfortable doing most of the talking.

The rain changed to delicate mist by the time school let out. Evangeline, Leeana, and I moseyed down Main Street. Mrs. Wilson scowled at us through the bakery windows; Mr. Johnson waved from the livery. The Chinese laundrymen were too busy to notice us.

At the next side street, Leeana stopped. "I'm going into the joss house to offer a prayer for my uncle. You can come with me if you want."

I felt a little shy about going into a Chinese church. I thought I would probably do something ignorant. The idea of evil spirits lurking nearby didn't offer any comfort, either. What if I made a mistake and tempted them? What if I somehow let them loose? What if I offended the guardian spirits that were supposed to protect folks? It felt safer to stay right where I was.

Leeana studied me with her questioning expression, the one that made me think I was being tested. Evangeline's eyes had grown to the approximate size of saucers.

Mama had told us often enough that we could pray anywhere and God was certain-sure to hear. I figured the Chinese temple couldn't be an exception to Mama's rule, and I really was glad to pray for Uncle Shoon.

"Sure," I said. "We'd like to come along."

We stood on the street in front of the joss house, considering the contrast between its curved curlicues and the tidy white picket fence. I imagined that the dragonfish stared down on us with as much curiosity about me as I felt about them. Evangeline snugged her hand into mine. Leeana took a cloth-wrapped bundle out of her lunch bucket and opened the gate.

We started down the slanty path, the one Leeana had said would confuse demons. I was entirely in favor of demons getting confused!

The plank porch made a hollow sound, like the bridge over Bunkum Creek. We passed between two red columns into an entryway that was painted bright blue. It was like walking into the sky.

Evangeline had to take a huge step to get over the high doorsill. I was looking at my feet, trying to get across without tripping and making a fool of myself. Evangeline gasped.

I glanced up and echoed her sentiments. We faced a screen covered with staring, widemouthed faces.

"It's only a spirit screen," Leeana said. "Once past it, we won't need to worry about demons."

I took a deep breath and wondered which was more frightening, the demons or the demon protection. Evangeline still held my hand. I took at least as much comfort from that as I gave.

The air was heavy with quiet and incense. We turned right, directly into a fat man with a white beard. Evangeline let out a little squeak.

He looked down at us with laugh-crinkled eyes and a smile as broad as a rainbow. I did feel foolish to realize he was yet another carved figure. A squat ceramic container, nearly full of sand, sat before him. Sticks stuck up from the sand like dead trees after a forest fire.

Leeana didn't let on if she noticed us getting jumpy over a piece of carved wood. She took three of the same kind of stick and a box of matches from her bundle.

"We must pay our respects to Dai Tze, who welcomes us to the temple." She struck a match, releasing fire and stink. Then she held each stick in turn to the flame.

"We burn three joss sticks: one for heaven, one for Earth, and one for all of humankind."

Heavy perfume sweetened the air. Leeana planted her incense sticks in the sand beside the others, took one step back, and bowed her head. Evangeline and I did the same. I imagined that the crinkled eyes of Dai Tze blinked in satisfaction.

Behind Dai Tze, carved screens and colorful banners caused a riot for our eyes. Each banner hung from a staff, and each was a marvel of red and gold silk. All of them, but one, were rectangular.

The center banner was a great cylinder with a long gold fringe along its bottom. Gold embroidery covered every bit of it, just as carving covered the spirit screen. I allowed it was the most amazing piece of fancywork of my entire experience. Glints of light danced from tiny mirrors that looked to be actually woven into the fabric. Even in the darkish room I could make out Chinese letters, flowers, and dragons. Maybe because of shadows, the dragons seemed to nod to us and swish their scaly tails.

"That's the King's Umbrella," Leeana said. "It stands for whichever god is being honored."

Statues grinned or frowned at us. One held a hand up, as if to give advice. Another's hands were folded peaceful-like, in his lap. A goddess stood in flowing robes with her hands raised up like a frozen-solid dancer. Her face was soft, and her expression tender as rosebuds.

Evangeline overcame her hesitation and dropped my hand. She gazed all around, then whispered, "How many gods do you have, anyway?"

Leeana watched us gape and smiled a private smile. I'm certain-sure she knew her answer would shock us.

"This is a Taoist temple. I don't think it's exactly like what you call a church. It's a meeting place, where the men come to discuss things and make decisions. Travelers come here for rest and help, too.

"It's true that we do worship here. I don't know exactly how many gods there are, but Uncle Shoon says there are as many as the grains of gold dust or as many as the stars."

She winked at Evangeline. "Personally, I think he exaggerates. There can't be more than twenty or thirty thousand."

Evangeline stared. "Thirty thousand!" She rolled the number in her mouth as if she could get a sense of its shape and size, but I doubted she could, for that number was far over my own reach.

Leeana chuckled at our amazement and went on explaining the King's Umbrella. "Those little mirrors protect us, too. Demons are so hideous that when they see their own reflection they get scared and run away."

"Sort of like the Wilson boys," Evangeline said. "They get grieved by seeing their own face on the other. That's why they're always in a bad mood."

Leeana guffawed then and clapped her hands. I felt a shiver. Was it truly allowed to laugh here? If all those demons and gods were lurking nearby, it seemed to me to be much more sensible to stay quiet. Evangeline laughed, too, but I determined myself to shut pan and not attract any unnecessary attention.

There was a whole lot more to see than to say, anyway. Leeana guided us along the wall to our left. We passed an altar with two statues of ladies in fine dresses. Leeana paused and bowed her head briefly before them. Evangeline did the same and I followed suit.

"These are the goddesses of childbirth and mercy,"

she said. "Kuan Yin is the goddess of mercy. She is *always* gentle, *always* kind."

The goddess called Kuan Yin was beautiful, with full, slightly curved lips and half-closed eyes. I thought it would not be hard to tell her of my most secret worries.

Someone had left fruit and flowers on a cloth-covered table. A few were fresh and still full of color; most were shriveled and brown. A jar of golden honey gleamed bright as sweet corn in August. Leeana unwrapped her bundle, revealing a red apple and a slightly wilted Gloriosa daisy. She placed them tenderly beside the others. I wondered what Mama would think about having her gifts passed on to Chinese gods.

Then she picked two wood blocks from the floor and knelt before a small altar. Evangeline knelt beside Leeana so naturally that I felt large and awkward standing beside them. So I knelt, too, and gazed up at the faces of two god figures.

"I will speak to the gods in English," Leeana's voice took on a respectful tone. "Please, Toy Sing Goon, doctor of ten thousand herbs, guide my mother's hands, and mine, as we care for Uncle Shoon. Show us how to help him to become well. Let him have strength. Let him have joy."

She turned to the figure beside Toy Sing Goon. "Please, Uah Poe, guide our hands and hearts to make good health. You know how to heal wounds and cure sickness. Please favor Uncle Shoon with your blessings."

I bowed my head and felt the majesty of the place. To my own God, whom I knew from church Sundays and family prayers, I also sent a plea for Uncle Shoon. My heart knew that Evangeline did the same.

Smack! I jumped when Leeana struck the blocks together, one, two, three times, then let them fall to the floor. One landed with its rounded side up, the other with the square side up. She gazed down at them and looked relieved.

"The signs are very good. They say Uncle Shoon will recover."

I was surprised to feel so much comfort from two ordinary pieces of wood, though I did allow that they might not be entirely ordinary. Whatever the cause, I was considerably more cheerful as we stepped over the high sill on our way out of the temple. Evangeline was unusually quiet, though. She didn't say a word the whole way through China Shacks to Leeana's house.

Mrs. Lee greeted us at the door. "Such good news! Uncle Shoon is sitting up and he says he is hungry. I think he will be better very soon."

Chapter 17

❖

EVANGELINE DID NOT volunteer a description of the joss house when we got home. At first I was grateful, for I feared all the talk of gods and demons would alarm Mama. Then I simply got used to silence on that subject and accepted it. *I* was not going to stir that pot. The straight-up truth is this: What I felt in the joss house was a lot like what I sometimes feel in our own church. Words would not do the feelings credit.

The week wore on, ordinary as vanilla pudding. Enough rain fell to keep water flowing to the mines. China Joe volunteered to make Mrs. Lee's deliveries. Every morning he was at her house, packing Buttermilk with fresh buns. Every afternoon he was there again, visiting Uncle Shoon. When we arrived after school on Friday, they were sitting together on the porch.

"Hello, Angels!" China Joe's voice was hearty.

Uncle Shoon smiled at us and murmured a hello.

He inclined his head and reached out his hand toward Leeana. She accepted it, then settled on the floor at his feet.

Mrs. Lee came out of the house carrying a teapot and two tiny bowls, which I recognized as Chinese teacups. Her steps had a little bounce, as if she were a kettle just warm enough to simmer and readying the boil. She offered her uncle a steaming cup of tea and adjusted the pillow behind his back.

Uncle Shoon held the hot cup with his thumb and index finger at the rim, supporting it from below with his little finger. He took a noisy sip and smacked his lips. Mrs. Lee hovered beside him, beaming.

They asked about how school had been and inquired after Mama's and Pa's health. China Joe told a story about a miner who lost his poke of gold in an outhouse.

"He searched his pockets mighty good and all around the floor, but there was no sign of his fortune. He used a lantern and peered down into the pit. Sure enough, his treasure was spilled across the heap below.

"So he ran *those* diggin's through the sluice box. He said he'd rather be a little disgusted than a lot poor." China Joe chuckled quietly, pleased by the telling of his story.

Evangeline whooped, but I tried not to smile too broadly, for the story concerned something my family didn't usually discuss. I did stash it in my mind for telling to Tom later, maybe omitting where I heard it.

A little silence followed, while we contemplated how we would have made that miner's choice. Leeana had been restless-seeming during the story. Now she shifted, drew a deep breath, and spoke up in her most respectful voice.

"Uncle Chou, there is no school tomorrow. I can deliver Mother's buns."

He considered her for a silent moment, as if he needed to be convinced that she could do the work required. Uncle Shoon looked solemn. Mrs. Lee stood quite still and a frown shadowed her face. Leeana directed her gaze at the porch floor, but I knew her well enough by then to see that she was impatient. Her eyes were obedient, but her tight lips threatened revolt.

Evangeline didn't let politeness hinder enthusiasm at all. "That sounds grand! Can we come along?"

My sister can be too fresh for my own mother's taste, and I was ready to scold her if need be. I looked quickly at Mrs. Lee's face, and saw the shadow lift.

"Oh, yes. That would be so kind. An Li would be happy to have your company. You must first ask for permission from your mother, of course. I hope she will say yes to you, because it is a good thing to feed the miners. They work hard, and they are very hungry."

China Joe and Uncle Shoon nodded silent agreement. Leeana jumped up and hugged her mother, shooting a sideways grin at Evangeline. I resolved to

convince Mama that we should spend Saturday helping Leeana.

"That sounds like work. You aren't so willing to work
around home lately. Why should you go off on a Saturday, when your own chores have piled up all week?"

Mama's words were stern, but her voice wasn't. I
knew she was right. It took all of us working together
to keep up the farm. I opened my mouth to make
promises, but Evangeline had already worked out her
argument. I shut pan and let her make it.

"We'll get up extra early, Mama. We'll do the milking and build the fire and have our bread rising before
you even get out of bed."

She raised up on her toes a bit to punctuate each
task, and her braids bounced on the words "early,"
"milking," "fire," and "bread." I wanted to smile, but I
was afraid I might ruin her speech. She went on, barely
pausing for her own breath, much less for interruptions
from me.

The sunny days were getting scarce, she explained,
sounding just enough like a grown-up. The rain would
be back soon. We owed a neighborly debt to the Lee
family because of their trouble and because Leeana
had chased away that bobcat. The miners "work hard
and they are very hungry." I smiled to myself at that,
for it did have a familiar ring.

Finally, she explained the biggest reason, but in a
casual way that made it almost sound unimportant. We

yearned to explore the diggin's along Bunkum Creek. Privately, I allowed that I also yearned to spend a day with Leeana.

We waited together for Mama's answer. We must have looked hopeful as cats at milking time, because she tilted her head back and laughed aloud.

"You start the bread and sweep the floors before you go. I guess I can spare two girls for one day. But you can only go tomorrow. I will have my whole family at church this Sunday."

This last was aimed my way, since I had spent the last Sabbath gallivanting. I vowed to be extra helpful to Mama in the future, for she did need our help and she was patient about our slothful inclinations. Meanwhile, I looked forward to a whole day with Leeana.

"Angelena. Wake up!" Evangeline must have some special way to tell time, for to me the world looked as black as midnight. Still, I stirred myself awake and we set about our chores.

Mama had laid the fire the night before, so all I had to do was put a match to it. I set the breakfast table while the room warmed and Evangeline swept the kitchen and porch. Pa and Tom came to the table and ate, with only a few words uttered in low tones. We all conspired to let Mama get some extra rest.

She came out of the bedroom, fussing with the ties to her big apron. Her eyes were so clear that I suspicioned she had been awake all along and couldn't bear to let Pa and Tom leave without a personal good-bye.

The distant sky was a paler shade of dark when they left for the diggin's. I coated our bread dough with a thin layer of butter, covered it with a damp cloth, and put it near the fire to rise. Evangeline cleared the table and washed up the breakfast dishes, making tiny sounds like a busy mouse.

Mama packed dinner pails for us to carry to Pa and Tom, and Jasper if he was working that day. She carefully placed cinnamon rolls on the top, where they wouldn't be crushed.

Whispering and giggling, we called a soft good-bye to Mama, for Reuben was still fast asleep. We raced down the hill and crossed the log bridge with careful haste. I expect we were on the edge of China Shacks before Mama's coffee was cool enough to drink.

Buttermilk waited beside Leeana's porch with his two huge baskets already loaded. Uncle Shoon sat on the bench. "Good morning, Angel Girls." His voice was still small, but larger than it had been the day before.

Mrs. Lee came out with her arms full. "I am so glad for you going with An Li. I'm sure that you will be lucky, all together."

It came to me that she would not have allowed Leeana to go alone. For some reason, she felt better having her daughter in our company. That made me proud, although I wasn't entirely sure why. I vowed to live up to Mrs. Lee's trust.

Leeana appeared in the doorway, carrying the small book bound in gold-embroidered red silk. It was the book of Chinese writing she had shared with Miss Jensen.

"I need to return this to Uncle Chou. We can visit him when we finish our deliveries." She tucked it deep within the fragrant basket of rolls, along with a plain black ledger book.

Mrs. Lee inspected the burro and its burden, tugging on straps and tucking cloth wrappers more snugly around the buns. She helped us attach the dinner buckets so they wouldn't clank and bother Buttermilk. As she worked, she talked to Leeana in Chinese. I didn't know the words, but she had an advice-giving look on her face.

The three of us set off with willing steps. Release from everyday duties lifted our spirits and spun them like whirligigs. A feather drifted toward us from a startled jay. Leeana plucked it from the air and nestled it between the pages of China Joe's book.

Half a mile out of town, the creek slowed to a wide shallow course. There we came upon China Flats and a group of miners already hard at work.

Pa said when he came to Bounty, Bunkum Creek was "wall-to-wall miners." Soon the easy gold was gone and full-time miners moved on, leaving great heaps of tailings behind. Pa's own claim had long ago been mined down to bedrock, so he and Tom were "drifting" into the hillside, hoping for richer deposits.

Chinese mostly worked the tailings in played-out mines. These Celestials were mining leftovers.

I counted five men. Two knelt beside the creek, filling buckets. They hung the buckets on long poles, which they balanced across their shoulders and then, with quick steps, carried to a wood rocker. A third man shoveled gravel from a great pile of tailings into the box. The last two grasped the rocker handles and tilted it up, then down, sloshing water and gravel around until the gold hidden within sank to the bottom.

Black felt hats shaded their faces with wide brims. Layers of shirts topped with dark sweaters protected them from the morning chill. They wore wide-legged denim pants and their feet were encased in heavy boots.

One of them saw us and said something to the others. They stopped work and stared as we approached. I guess they weren't accustomed to seeing three girls and a burro up in the diggin's.

One of the men who had been working the rocker stepped forward and bobbed his head in greeting. His voice was plenty loud, but it didn't matter for he was speaking in Chinese. His gestures made us welcome, though. I thought he never would give over his little bows, and his companions were the same. They shifted from foot to foot and nodded welcomes to us.

Evangeline's easy friendliness soon distributed smiles all around. Her spirited bowing made her braids dance.

After what seemed to me like a lot of talk, Leeana handed them a wrapped bundle of pork buns. They paid her in moonlight-pale gold dust, carefully measured out on a balance scale, and tucked into Leeana's gold poke. I knew it was local gleanings, for Pa says our dust here in Bounty has a lot of silver mixed in with it. Our nuggets are peculiar, too. They're large, but right squashed-looking, as if someone had taken a hammer to them.

Leeana recorded the purchase and payment in her ledger book. She wrote Chinese characters under the watchful gaze of the headman. Finally, he clucked approval and, with another flurry of bobbing bows, we proceeded on our way.

Chapter
18
❖

WE WOUND THROUGH the forest edge because the flats were so rocky. Pebbles rolled underfoot dangerously. The burro needed sound footing, and I speculated that this might have been how Uncle Shoon got thrown.

"I'll wager Buttermilk slipped on these loose rocks when your uncle was hurt."

Leeana fussed with the burro's baskets, moving some of the buns to the side opposite the heavy gold. She didn't answer.

The next diggin's was Poorman's Flat, where our riding party had watched the Celestials hydraulicking. These men were as welcoming as the others, but I was right mystified to hear Leeana speaking a kind of simple English.

On the way to the next stop, I asked, "Why didn't you talk Chinese to those men?"

"China is very large and people there speak many different languages. Sometimes we have to use English to understand each other."

That was an amazement to me for I had thought all Chinese was the same. Still, there was more to my puzzlement. She had written in her book with Chinese characters.

"If you don't speak the same language, how can you read the same language?"

I felt the more I knew, the less I understood, but the answer turned out to be simple and sensible.

"Character writing isn't like English, where you sound out the words. Each symbol stands for an idea, or a thing, or sometimes an action. No matter what language a person speaks, the written language is the same."

Evangeline paid very little attention to us. She petted Buttermilk and chattered to the miners. She admired autumn butterflies and watched pileated woodpeckers as they swooped overhead, calling in rusty voices.

Buttermilk's load grew lighter in buns, and heavier in gold. We worked our way downstream, crossing the creek twice to reach claims on either side.

Just upstream from Pa's claim, we found a broad shallow spot with boulders that poked above the water. Evangeline grabbed Pa's and Tom's dinner buckets and I took Jasper's. We scrambled and jumped from one rock to the next, and reached the other side of

Bunkum Creek without dampening so much as a toe. Leeana stayed on the west bank.

"I'll wait here for you," she said, and settled on a sun-warmed rock.

Tom saw us first and whistled a greeting. They were mighty glad for the dinner pails, and I think they were glad to see us, too, for Pa hugged us both and showed us where they had tunneled into the bank. Jasper looked puzzled, though, for he had not heard of our plan.

When we explained, he lowered his brow down over his eyes and peered upstream to where Leeana and Buttermilk rested.

"I can't believe your ma would let you keep company with no dang Chinee," he said at last. "I always thought she had more sense than that."

"Leeana isn't a dang Chinee!" Evangeline was indignant. "She's our friend."

"Simmer down, Jasper. They're just trying to help a neighbor." Tom shot a warning look Jasper's way and put his dinner bucket down. "Come on, girls. We'll give you a ride."

"Neighbor!" Jasper spat on the ground and glared at Tom, but he did simmer down.

Jasper and Tom mounted Pug and Majesty and helped us up to ride behind them. They carried us dry-footed back across the creek. Leeana saw us coming and put on her company manners. She stood beside Buttermilk with her hands at her sides and her eyes aimed at her feet. I understood that she was being polite, but I was sorry she didn't treat Jasper a bit more like a bobcat.

I introduced her to my brother and uncle. Tom was polite enough, dismounting and muttering a hello while he shuffled his feet in the dirt. Jasper inspected Buttermilk boldly, peering into the baskets. If he noticed the gold poke, he didn't let on. He leaned over and spat tobacco on the ground, making a mess right at Leeana's feet.

"I just wanted to be sure my nieces are in good company. It isn't really fitting for girls to go around the diggin's alone. They could get into trouble."

Leeana's eyes glinted, but she bobbed her head in a way I knew was courteous among her people. It just seemed to irritate Jasper. He had taken to carrying a riding quirt tucked into his boot. He pulled it out and sat tall astride Pug, tapping the little whip against his left palm.

"Some kinds of girls don't mind a little trouble. It sort of depends what kind of mother they have." *Tap! Tap!* "I hear your mother has lots of gentlemen around most days." *Tap! Tap!* "You take care you don't let nothing like that rub off on my nieces."

He raised the quirt and slapped Buttermilk on the rump. Buttermilk jerked back and tried to bolt, but Leeana was holding tight. She dug in her heels and held the little burro.

I was shocked speechless, but Evangeline shrieked, "You stop that!"

Tom put a restraining hand on Jasper's arm. "I swan, you've got a mouth on you. Come on. Pa needs us."

Leeana tugged Buttermilk's lead and strode up the path right smartly. From the set of her jaw and the stiffness in her shoulders, I considered she was right wrathy, and I didn't blame her. Jasper's words had been poison. His hitting Buttermilk was downright dangerous. It still puzzled me to see that mean streak in my uncle. It seemed he was nothing at all like Mama. I was plenty glad to see him riding back across the creek with Tom.

Evangeline and I hurried after Leeana and I tried to think of some way to apologize for my uncle. *Uncle.* It seemed odd even to use that word, for it meant something so different to the two of us.

Evangeline was out of breath from hurrying, but she managed to call out to Leeana. "Don't you pay Jasper any mind. He's just jealous because you're our friend."

I didn't know if Jasper was jealous or not, but I realized she was right about the second part. When we finally caught up with Leeana and Buttermilk, I had both the words and the determination to say them.

"Leeana."

She turned to me, still rigid with anger.

"Leeana, I can't fathom why, but Jasper is full of all

sorts of meanery. I can't help what *he* says or thinks, but I hope you'll let me be your friend."

She softened then, all over. Her face and shoulders and even her voice went gentle. "Thank you," she said. "Me, too."

The sun was high by the time we reached the place where Bunkum Creek flowed into the mighty Rogue. Deer Island was like a green stone set in precious silver. Up under the oaks and manzanita, China Joe sat on his front steps. His two cats napped beside him in the sun. As soon as he saw us trudging up the road, he waved a wide-grinned hello.

"Welcome, Angels! I have made a feast for the hungry travelers."

His tiny cabin was tidy and plain, furnished with only a cot, a small table with two chairs, a stove, a shelf holding cooking gear, and a bookcase. Half a dozen books stood on the bookcase beside a green statue. Two pictures of children and a steamship schedule were nailed to the wall. I stole a close look and saw that the schedule was for ships going from San Francisco to China.

China Joe brought in two rickety stools so all four of us could sit around the table for our feast. And it was, indeed, a feast. He had cooked a Chinese meal of rice and carrots, fancied up with smoked salmon and ginger. Of course, we ended the meal with plain buns and honey.

Our host settled back and lit his pipe, pulling the tobacco-flavored smoke in slowly, then letting it drift out into a fragrant cloud around his head. He closed his eyes for a moment like a blissful cat. He reminded me of Pa, who enjoyed the same ritual after a satisfying meal.

"Your honey is very good," Evangeline said. "It tastes like flowers."

"You are too kind to praise my poor offering," he said.

I had come to know that the Chinese are extra modest, so this didn't surprise me. We all knew the honey was excellent.

"Honey is lucky," he added. He regarded the jar on the table as if it were a unique and fascinating object.

"Consider. It is gold, a color very much valued in this place. It is sweet. It is beautiful, and it gives good health and prosperity."

"I saw honey in the joss house yesterday," Evangeline told him. "Did you leave it there?"

He didn't even look surprised. "Why, yes, I did. I was very worried about my friend. I went to the temple to ask the gods for guidance."

"We don't have all those gods, you know," Evangeline said in a confiding tone. "We figure one is enough."

China Joe inhaled deeply on his pipe and let out a long puff of smoke before he answered. "We believe there are many ways to the truth. We go to the temple to think about the right way to live."

Another puff, slowly exhaled. "A man must honor his neighbors. He must live thoughtfully to keep harmony in the universe. The gods direct us to practice humanity toward each other every day."

"You mean like the Golden Rule?"

"Explain your rule of gold, Second Angel. I don't know about that."

"Well, we are supposed to treat other people the way we want to be treated."

He beamed. "Just so. It is the same idea. The Taoists say, 'Why should I reject the way of your church? Gold and jade do not harm each other; crystal and amber do not make each other cheap.'"

It reminded me of Leeana's poem and I said, "Jade can't tarnish gold."

China Joe grinned at me. "Exactly."

"Is this jade?"

Evangeline had spotted the statue on the bookshelf. She rose and picked it up before I could stop her. I opened my mouth, but China Joe held out a hand, palm forward, to keep me from saying anything.

"Kuan Yin has been in human hands for many centuries. She will keep herself safe."

We watched Evangeline admire the little goddess and I did admit she held it as tenderly as a newborn kitten. This little figure of Kuan Yin had as much kindness and grace as her larger statue in the joss house.

"Isn't she beautiful?"

I took the goddess from Evangeline. Cool jade caught the light and shone like green water in sunlight. She was about eight inches tall, a slender lady whose head turned so her chin touched her left shoulder. A half-opened fan in her right hand contrasted with robes that flowed like liquid silk. I hardly dared to touch her, but she was so serene that I found myself believing she truly would come to no harm. I returned her to her safe place on the bookcase.

Leeana spoke briefly in Chinese and held out the gold-embroidered book. China Joe placed it on the shelf with as much care as I had taken with the statue. He picked up another and gave it to Leeana.

"I think you are ready for this one," he said in English.

She accepted the new book and bowed. It reminded me of how we always say, "Yes, ma'am," to Miss Jensen. It should have been plain to me all along. China Joe was not just Leeana's friend. He was her teacher.

"Who are they?"

Evangeline was inspecting two pictures tacked to the wall beside his bookshelf. They were of Chinese children, but they weren't photographs. They appeared to come from a newspaper.

China Joe stared at the pictures for a long moment, then shrugged and spoke. His voice was full of sorrow and sweetness.

"They are just children. I miss having children underfoot. I hope someday to return to China, to join my wife and have my own children. For now, the pictures remind me of my home and the days of my youth, before I came to Gum San."

"Gum San?" Evangeline's voice was a soft echo.

"The land of the Golden Mountain. That is what my people call America. It is a treasure place for us, a place to prosper so we can go home again with full pockets, so we can have enough wealth to feed our families."

"That's not so different from why our grandfather came to America," I said to Evangeline. "It's the land of opportunity for everyone."

The autumn sun told us we needed to start home. We left with Buttermilk's baskets empty of buns, but filled with the heavy pouch of gold, the new book for Leeana, and two jars of honey for Mama. We left China Joe standing on his top step with his cats winding figure eights around his legs.

Chapter 19

❖

EVANGELINE MUST HAVE CARRIED a considerable burden of thought concerning our visit to the joss house. It took her nearly a week to talk about it. When at last she did choose to talk, she caused a flat-out ruckus.

It was on Sunday morning while we walked to church. Tom had taken Majesty on an errand, and Pa said that Turnip deserved a day of rest. Our church was not too far distant, only a little way down Apple Street from the boardinghouse. We took turns carrying little Reuben.

Evangeline chattered about our outing with Leeana, giving special emphasis to the pleasures of Buttermilk's companionship.

"I'm glad you had a good time, Evangeline. Perhaps all that activity will help you keep still in church this morning. Your behavior isn't always suitable to the house of God."

Mama's chiding was almost automatic, but it was as if Evangeline had been waiting for just such a remark. She capped the climax and spoke what was truly on her mind.

Looking up at Mama with her head tilted and her nose wrinkled, as if she were trying out an idea that didn't quite fit, she said, "They make lots of noise in Leeana's church."

She paused. Then, in a voice as distinct as thunder on a dry day, she added, "And they have lots of different gods."

Mama stopped walking and stared in a silence that I recognized as dangerous. Evangeline rushed on to explain in more detail than I thought was strictly necessary.

"There's one for health and one for good luck and one for families. And Mama . . ." Her tone turned secret-quiet. "I think that one is in charge of making babies."

That was more than even I had counted on. Mama broke her silence in a rush.

"That's enough of that talk, miss. The First Commandment assures us that there is only one true God. If the Celestials have other opinions, we can only hope they come to their senses soon."

Reuben squirmed in Pa's arms and Mama reached for him. The moment had passed. Evangeline shut pan, a little late for my taste, and we crossed the bridge into town. I hoped the noise of our crossing would keep demons, if there be such, at bay.

During the service that morning, I clenched my eyes shut, trying to squeeze extra strength into my prayers.

"Please, God, can't we let Leeana and her people be? Why do they have to be exactly like us? And please, God, please, let Evangeline learn to keep her mouth shut now and then."

After Sunday dinner, Mama took off her apron and sat at the table. Indicating the two chairs opposite, she said, "Angelena, Evangeline, please sit down. I need to talk to you."

Pa came in and joined us, as if there had been some kind of signal between them. Tom stomped up the porch steps and, seeing us gathered there, came in to see what was happening. I stared at my hands in my lap. I had hoped church services and the meal would calm Mama, but she looked as grim as ever I had seen her. Pa lit his pipe.

"Angelena, tell me how Evangeline has been picking up these outlandish notions. Where did she get this idea that there could be more than one God?"

In spite of the fact that the question had been directed to me, Evangeline was extra willing to assist Mama's understanding.

"Oh, the joss house is plumb full of gods. The Celestials have as many gods as there are stars in the sky and each one helps with a different kind of problem."

"Whatever does she mean, Angelena?"

Mama's tone was mild, and I knew she was in one of her dangerous calms again. From the look on Evangeline's face, I knew that she finally realized this might be precarious ground. I was left to answer.

"They just do things their own way, Mama. Their temple is really a kind of general church and meeting place. It has some odd-seeming things in it, but lots of their ideas are the same as ours."

"Like the Golden Rule," Evangeline offered. "China Joe explained they have the same idea as we do about that."

"We were just talking with him, Mama. You remember China Joe. He sent that lovely honey."

"I remember the honey very well, Angelena, but I do not remember your telling me about any discussion of religion. Will you please tell me now?"

"China Joe was just explaining that the joss house is for all people and that they believe in the Golden Rule same as us."

"Except it's not at all like our church." Evangeline was too far away for me to kick her, Golden Rule or not.

"It's got a god who guards the door and says welcome, and it's got a god in charge of money and one in charge of getting well when you've been sick, and there's an altar for giving gifts. Leeana gave the doctor god an apple and one of the flowers you sent, so her uncle Shoon would get well. Sure enough, when we got back to her house, he was sitting up and acting oh-so-much better. They make just gobs of noise. They burn incense and bang gongs to call the gods so they will listen and . . ."

Mama's lips entirely lost their lovely fullness and straightened into a narrow line. Tom stared at Evangeline with horror. Then he glared at me.

I guessed he was blaming me for allowing our little sister to fall into heathen hands, as if anyone could allow or deny anything to Evangeline.

Pa listened in silence at first, but Evangeline's description of the inside of the joss house moved him to speak. "Do you mean you have been going inside the joss house in China Shacks and worshiping there?" His razor voice cut through Evangeline's chatter.

I tried to explain. "We did go into the joss house, Pa, but it was only to be with Leeana when she prayed for her uncle. We didn't exactly worship there."

Mama stood up. She didn't show any excitement at all; she looked and sounded serene as a stone. I guessed that meant she was stone-firm in her decisions.

"I'm afraid Chinese ideas are not good for you, Angelena, and I am certain they are not good for Evangeline. I'm sorry for Mrs. Lee's trouble, but you said yourself that her uncle is getting well."

"Oh, yes, ma'am. Leeana gave special gifts to the healing god, so Uncle Shoon is lots better." Evangeline would not keep still and I had stopped worrying about shushing her. It was too late to do any good.

Mama went on. "I would rather you take the other way to school. I'm sure Mrs. Lee will understand, even though her daughter may not."

"Yes, ma'am," I said, as yielding as goose down. "I'll explain it to Leeana tomorrow morning."

My mind was already inventing the polite-like lie that would save Leeana's feelings. *Mama thinks the log is dangerous, especially with all the rain we've been having.* That might do.

Mama wants us to stop by the Gustafsons' for Sarah. That would require extra explanation, for Sarah already had plenty of company on her way to school.

Mama wants us to help with the milking so we have to leave later. No. I could always get up a little earlier for milking.

Mama's afraid. She thinks your religion will corrupt us. I knew that was the straight-up truth, and yet it wouldn't do at all. I'd have to lie or hurt my friend, and it did occur to me to wonder how it all fit together. Hadn't Mama taught me to be kind, and hadn't she taught me never to lie? It couldn't be both ways. I sought some way to make the truth less hurtful. Mama solved my problem in an awful way.

"No, Angelena. She'll understand when you don't come for her tomorrow morning. China Shacks is full of strangers and strange doings. You mustn't ever go near there again, unless an adult is with you."

Pa leaves a lot of the talking to Mama, but now and again he makes a speech. He made one then.

"We build our lives on faith, family, and the farm. We believe in one true God, and we help each other. The townsfolk don't take kindly to your keeping company with a Celestial and we have to pay some attention to that, too. Miners can move on, but farmers have to live in a community."

He rose and stood beside Mama. "You have to build your own future with your own kind. I don't want to hear of you putting yourself or your sister in any kind of danger, from Celestial ideas or other folks. God gave you sense, Angelena. Use it."

Without another word, he went outside, indicating that Tom should follow. Tom did, still scowling. Evangeline looked sick. I thought it served her right, being that she had caused all the trouble with her mouth.

Chapter 20

IT RAINED HARD the next morning, and I was honestly glad not to test the log when it was soaked. Evangeline and I wore oiled canvas slickers to keep the rain off, but nothing could keep the wet off our feet. Smoke rising from the schoolhouse told us that Tony and Miss Jensen had fired up the stove, and we were glad for the promise of warmth.

Miss Jensen rang the first bell, then the second. Liza and I started our spelling drill, each of us taking a turn to test the other. I looked toward the door now and then while I waited for Liza to puzzle out a word.

At last, the door swung open and Leeana entered, with her dark hair hanging in waterlogged strands. Rain dripped from her nose. Her uncle's gum boots were caked with clingy mud. She glanced my way first off, casually, as if she didn't actually expect for me to be there. When her eyes met mine, the puzzlement on her face broke my heart.

She hung her quilted cotton jacket by the fire and sank onto the bench beside me, quaking with cold and wet. I offered her my sweater, but she shook her head with a quick motion and bent to study her book.

Rain battered the windowpanes, sometimes wind-driven so hard that it boomed against the glass. We had been so confined that Miss Jensen said we could clear the back of the schoolroom at lunch and play circle games.

Liza might have liked being the biggest toad in the puddle overmuch, but I allow she was good at organizing fun. Like lightning, she had the boys moving benches aside and herded everyone into a big, cheerful circle. She made no effort to include Leeana, but she didn't snub her, either. It appeared to be Leeana's choice to join Miss Jensen at the other end of the room. They talked in earnest while the rest of us went through hilarious rounds of "Farmer in the Dell."

Lunch over, we assembled for afternoon lessons. Leeana spoke to me at last.

"I was afraid you might be sick. My mother worried, too."

"I'm sorry, Leeana," I whispered. All the lies flew out of my head. "Mama says we aren't to go to your house anymore."

She showed no sign of the anger I had feared. The tiniest of smiles caressed her lips. She answered me gently.

"I know you have tried to be my friend." That was all she would say.

She worked in her book and practiced spelling with Evangeline and Sarah Gustafson. She studied quietly until the school day was over. Then she carried her books up to Miss Jensen and bowed to her.

I waited. If I couldn't go to her house, at least I could talk to her at school. But she went the other way, around the edge of the room, and just when I was going to go after her, Liza grabbed my arm.

"Sarah told her mama and she told Mrs. Wilson how that Chinee girl tried to force you to worship false gods. That was enough for Mrs. Wilson. She and Mr. Wilson talked to the town council and the town council talked to Miss Jensen. Good riddance to bad rubbish is what I say. It's scary to think how close you came to losing your immortal soul to heathen ways of worship."

She rolled her eyes broadly toward heaven and then at me. "You must feel a mite scared to have had such a close call with demons."

Looking into Liza's eager eyes, I wasn't so all-fired sure I had escaped.

Leeana wasn't at school the next day, nor the next. At first I tried to convince myself that she had caught a cold from her drenching, but by Friday I understood that she truly would not be back. On Friday afternoon, Miss Jensen asked me to stay with her for a moment after school.

"I know you and Leeana are close. You were the first one to accept her and offer your friendship. I wonder if you would take a book to her. I don't want her to fall behind in her reading."

She handed me a book about Thomas Jefferson. I opened it and saw *Mary Jensen* written on the inside of the cover. It was one of her personal books.

She obviously didn't know I had been forbidden to go to China Shacks. I considered how I might deliver the book. I didn't dare to disobey Mama, so I must not go to Leeana's house. Still, I felt a need to tell her I was sorry for many things. Well, maybe I wouldn't tell her precisely that I had once thought she was too ignorant to read English.

"I'll take it to her." The book felt heavy in my hand.

I talked to Mama that night.

"They won't let her in school anymore, Mama, and she hasn't done anything wrong. It isn't fair! They blame her just for being what she is."

Mama's silence wasn't dangerous this time. She made it easy for me to talk, leaning toward me and seeming to listen with her whole body. I think she especially listened with her heart.

"You say she reads well."

"Yes, but she has to miss all the geography and arithmetic. She can't learn proper American ways if she isn't ever allowed to be around regular people."

"What do you want to do?"

"I just want to be her friend. I want to be able to spend time with her sometimes and help her learn how we do things in America. Folks are so mean to her, but she's only been kind to me and Evangeline."

At that her lips tightened just a bit. "I can't let you take Evangeline. She's too young to sort out all the confusion about gods and customs. But if you will do your chores early and late, you may visit with Leeana on Saturday."

"Oh, Mama, thank you. I hate to see her so all alone."

Mama put her arm around my shoulder in a hug that mixed teasing and fondness. "It's fine with me if your reason is simple friendship. You don't have to have a noble reason for everything you do."

Then she looked serious as a sermon. "Angelena, be careful when you are with Leeana. I expect you're old enough to keep yourself from most harm, but there is no knowing what people will do if they feel threatened and righteous at the same time. Some of the local folks aren't as full of charity as you."

"I wouldn't go near China Shacks, Mama. I would just meet Leeana on the trail and talk with her. Miss Jensen wants me to take this book to her and I need to explain how Evangeline is too young to understand about different ways of faith. She likes Evangeline, Mama. She would never do her harm. And, Mama, she can't do me harm. I'm old enough to tell sense from nonsense."

"I can't protect you forever, and we do owe courtesy and kindness to the Lees. But you must stay away from China Shacks entirely. I hear there's an opium den there, and lots of miners are drifters. We don't know what they might do."

I had to grant her that, but didn't we have a gambling saloon right in town, and weren't some white miners drifters? I thought her worry was deeper than her words, and it had somewhat to do with Mrs. Wilson and her threats. I wondered if it had to do with Jasper.

It was easy to push worry aside with anticipation. On Saturday morning, I set out early. Evangeline watched me go with sad eyes, but there was no question of her going along. Mama had been firm about that, and I was glad, for I wanted to talk with Leeana alone.

I followed the west bank of Bunkum Creek toward our diggin's, to the shallow spot with the boulder crossing. It was quick work to gain the other side and settle on the rock Leeana had used when she waited for us the week before. A fist-sized chunk of pink quartz caught my eye. Quartz is pretty, and the miners say the pink kind is a sure sign of gold. I sat on the rock, studying the faint pink streaks and enjoying the tranquility.

A muted shout interrupted the quiet. Pa wasn't working the diggin's that day, so I was surprised to see Jasper and Tom, coming up the other side. Moving fast astride their horses, they didn't notice me at all. About fifty yards downstream, they splashed across. I jumped up to see where they were going and stepped off the path without looking down.

Whirrrr.

A shiver fluttered up my spine and perched at the base of my neck. I stood as rigid as ice. That sound was unmistakable.

Whirrr.

Rustling dry leaves can fool you into thinking there's a rattler nearby. So can crickets, sometimes. But a real rattler sounds like only one thing . . . a rattler.

Chapter 21

I MOVED only my eyes. There it was, behind the log, a dun-colored coil nearly invisible against the dappled beige of dry grass in shadow.

It's not my nature to be brave. I fancy flight over fight most times. But I had seen Leeana stare down a bobcat and watched her stand up to hateful folks. I drew in a long breath, steadying my aim, and hurled the rock at the snake's head.

Thump! A direct hit. The snake thrashed sideways. I ducked down to grab another rock. *Thump!* It smacked the ground right behind the absquatulating rattler.

"Wowee! You showed him who's boss!" It was Leeana.

I turned, delighted that she had seen my triumph. "I'm glad to see you," I said. "I was on my way to find you."

Leeana grinned. She and Buttermilk stood on the path, familiar as sunshine. "I'm glad to see you, too."

"Miss Jensen sent this." I offered the book.

She read the gold print on its back, forming words in a soft whisper.

"*Letters of Thomas Jefferson.*" She slipped the book into a deep pocket of her quilted cotton jacket. "I can start it after chores tonight. Did she say when I should bring it back?"

"No. She didn't say much. She had to sort of sneak it to me after school."

"Thank her for her kindness," Leeana murmured. Then, changing the subject, she picked two more rocks from the path and put them into the other pocket, where they made an irregular bulge. "Snake repellent."

It was good to laugh together.

I described what had happened at school that week while we strolled up the trail. Buttermilk followed like a patient dog.

"Miss Jensen told us all about a place called Germany and all the rivers there. She drew it on the big chalkboard and taught us names like Rhine and Rhone, and one she called Dan-you, but she spelled it with a *B*."

"The Wilsons came from Germany," Leeana said. "They talk like they're trying to spit." She giggled into her open palm and tipped her head back. "They say we talk funny, but I guess we don't spell Dan-you with a *B*."

"As far as I can tell, 'most everybody talks funny," I said. "Those men up at Kanaka Flat talk in something called Hawaiian. I never could figure out where that was."

"Way out in the ocean, somewhere, I think. My mother said the ship that brought her across stopped there. They wouldn't let her out, though. They just filled up with water and supplies and kept on going."

"My folks came across the Oregon Trail when they were kids. That was only grass and mountains, with a few rivers here and there. I'd be scared to go so far over water. How long did it take?"

"Many weeks. That's all my mother says. Many weeks." Her voice dropped to a whisper. "She doesn't like to talk about it."

Sadness settled on her. I tried to think of something to say that would lift her spirits. "Maybe you can come back to school soon. With the rainy season on us, the Wilson boys will be at the diggin's to work with their dad. They're the cause of most of the meanness. The rest of the kids don't mind your being there so much."

"The rest of the kids mind." Leeana's voice was carefully flat. "They say the gold is disappearing because of us."

I wanted to object, but couldn't think of a way to do it. That was exactly what the Wilsons and Liza said, and especially Jasper. Even Tom said the Chinese would be happier back home in China.

I couldn't think of anything positive to say right then, so I followed Mama's advice and shut pan.

We visited a few claims, both white and Chinese, where Leeana sold her mother's buns and collected yellow gold dust. We kept a gentle pace, lingering to watch a deer step daintily into the deep woods. We stopped by a huge boulder that stood half in and half out of a deep section of the creek, and watched the water dance.

I picked up a handful of gravel. One by one I launched the pebbles into a deep pool. The plunk and splash emphasized the words I had rehearsed.

"I'm sorry, Leeana. I hope you understand. My parents're trying to protect Evangeline. Your people's ideas are strange to them, and she's so young."

"I know. They're afraid."

I wanted to say that wasn't so. I didn't, because it was clear that it *was* so.

I changed the subject. "There's going to be a fiddle contest and bake sale for the school. Your mother would be a shoo-in for a prize. I wish you would come."

"You know we can't," Leeana said, "at least not till this trouble passes."

The moving water whispered against the rock. Talk started to flow slowly, then easily, like the water. Leeana settled against the sun-warmed granite and we kept to safer subjects.

I was at the funniest part of a story about a goat that followed the Wilson boys to school and ate a good portion of Liza's new straw hat when I was startled by a sharp crack. Buttermilk tried to bolt, but Leeana held him fast. It had sounded like a gigantic whip snapping. Gunshots!

Leeana and I ducked behind the boulder. Something big crashed through the underbrush downstream. Dogs barked. Men yelled. I peered around the rock and saw a small man break through a willow thicket. He wore dark pants and a loose white shirt. His long braid bounced as he dropped from the bank into the cold water. The current caught him and he went under, then surfaced, sputtering and thrashing.

His tormentors gathered at the water's edge. Two dogs dove in and swam in excited circles, yelping.

One of the figures raised a rifle and fired carelessly in the direction of the swimming man. The gun sounded and the dogs replied, raising the pitch of their yaps and yowls to a new level of clamor as the man reached the opposite shore and scampered into the underbrush.

"I guess that shows us what the Wilson boys are doing for fun." Leeana's voice brimmed with bitterness. "All told, I'd rather meet with rattlesnakes."

"It's just rattlesnakes with human skin," I observed, matching her bitterness.

I felt helpless and sad, knowing I had the personal acquaintance of the snakes. The man who fired the last shot had been Jasper. Worse, Tom was up on the bank watching it all.

The Celestial stayed hidden. The riders left, probably to find some new kind of meanery. They rode downstream, still laughing and firing gunshots into the air. Leeana never mentioned Jasper or Tom, and I was ashamed to realize that I hoped she didn't recognize them.

We followed slowly, staying far behind. At the next two diggin's, the miners jumped at every loud noise. Although they treated Leeana with their usual courtesy, they did not look at me and would not speak to me. It was a relief to get back on the trail.

Trying to get the conversation going again, I chattered about anything that came to mind. I started to talk about our school's usual winter entertainments, but when I got to Miss Jensen's plans for a Christmas pageant, I feared that Leeana might not understand.

"Do you know about Christmas?"

"Oh, yes. Your god came to earth to teach all persons to love one another."

I couldn't think of a single thing to add to that.

We reached the river and headed downstream toward Deer Island and China Joe's cabin. Buttermilk sensed that we were near our destination, for he trotted a bit and we had to trot, too, to keep up. We arrived at the cabin out of breath and ready for a rest.

"Uncle? I brought my friend," Leeana said. I found my heart pleased to hear that word again from her lips. "Uncle?"

The cats emerged from under the cabin. One meowed plaintively at the door. One came to sit square in front of me as if it expected me to do something. It watched my face in a way that made me uneasy. What did it want?

Leeana knocked on the door. Still there was no answer. We looked among the beehives. China Joe was nowhere.

"Mother sent you pork buns and steamed cakes." This time Leeana pushed gently on the cabin door. It creaked open.

The once tidy room was a jumble of overturned furniture, heaped with clothing and topped with books lying open like startled birds. Leeana backed out of the cabin, almost knocking me down the steps.

She called out in Chinese and ran down to the river's edge, the only place we hadn't searched.

"There!" I spotted cloth shoes and cuffless denim pants partly hidden by a shrubby willow.

Leeana reached him first. She moaned his name and knelt beside him, stroking his head. He might have been asleep but for the red stain in the middle of his shirt.

She called his name over and over, but no answer was possible. He was dead.

Chapter
22

❖

IT WAS LIKE standing on the edge of a cliff, with nothing before me but vast space, and behind me the cold pushing force of some unknown person's hatred.

Leeana sat among the damp rocks with China Joe's head cradled in her lap. I knelt beside her, afraid to touch him, but desperate to do something that would make the horror go away. Feeling helpless, I put my arm around Leeana. She shuddered and nestled her head against my shoulder, then began to sob.

At last she wiped at her tears with her sleeve and sat upright. I recognized the bobcat fighter in her straight spine. She said, "We must get help. We have to take him back to town, so the proper ceremonies can be done for him."

She gently laid China Joe's head back upon the rounded stones. As she did so, I saw a short stub of black hair at the nape of his neck. Someone had cut off his queue.

We had no choice but to leave him there just a little longer. We hastened to the closest diggin's and told the miners what we had found. China Joe had friends in every camp. Their reaction was shock and sorrow, and fear.

A kind old Celestial walked back to Bounty with me and Leeana. Three others went to fetch China Joe. Buttermilk carried that dreadful burden back to town.

I left Leeana and her escort at the log bridge and climbed the hill to home. I must have been a sight, for Evangeline gaped when I entered the house. Mama glanced my way when she heard me come in, then dropped her stirring spoon and rushed to fold me in her arms. I stayed there willingly.

Evangeline fetched Pa from his work in the barn, and they gathered close around.

"He was dead, Mama. The cats were so confused, and when we finally did find him, he was dead."

Mama didn't hush me, even though Evangeline was wide-eyed with the terrible news. She just held me in a tight embrace and whispered, "Tell us about it, Ange-lena. Telling helps."

So I described the ransacked cabin and how we had searched for China Joe. I told them how Leeana had cried, and how the miners had reacted when we brought the bitter news. Finally, I told them about China Joe's missing queue.

Pa and Mama listened, murmuring now and then in sympathy. Reuben was silent, for though he didn't understand what had happened, he did understand that it was serious. The hardest face to look at was Evangeline's.

"It isn't fair." She sounded bewildered. "He was just an old man. What will his bees do now? What will happen to his cats?"

Mama held me.

We were gathered like that when Tom and Jasper came in. Jasper was full of questions concerning what I had seen. Tom was full of silence. When I told them how China Joe had been murdered, I admit to looking extra close at Jasper. Hadn't I seen him shooting toward a Chinese miner just an hour before we found China Joe?

"It was a murder, sure and simple," I said, determined to see if he looked scared or concerned.

Tom was the one who surprised me. He appeared to be trying on Jasper's attitudes. "What in tarnation were you doing there? I thought you were forbidden to go near those Celestials!"

"I gave her special permission, Tom. She wasn't doing any harm." Mama stroked my hand, then squeezed it gently.

Pa spoke to Tom most directly. "It doesn't concern you, does it?"

Tom hung his head and didn't answer, but Jasper couldn't help but say what he felt. "It concerns any self-respecting American. She oughtn't be consorting with heathens. And as for the dang Chinee, they shouldn't

152

expect anything else as long as they keep stealing white man's gold."

Then, like a donkey determined to go south when the farmer is traveling north, he added, "Besides that, there isn't such a thing as murdering a Chinaman. Chinee don't count when it comes to killing."

Tom didn't volunteer any comments about the Chinese, but he did say I shouldn't have been out at the diggin's, where "anything could happen."

It seemed to me that "anything" *had* happened.

I thought about Leeana and Mrs. Lee. How would they manage without China Joe? I thought about Uncle Shoon, too. I could find no way to believe now that he had been thrown by gentle Buttermilk.

Even in extraordinary times, ordinary life continues. We went to church on Sunday, and on Monday, Evangeline and I went to school, as usual. After lunch, we were doing pairs and I was helping Evangeline with spelling. "Doubtful." I held the slate close so she couldn't see the spelling.

"Doubtful. D . . . O . . . U . . ." Evangeline hesitated. I thought Leeana would have been amused. Here was yet another word with a misplaced *b*. I waited, trying not to give eye messages to my sister.

"B." She glanced at me to see if I would offer a clue. I must have, for she went on with confidence. "T . . . F . . . U . . . L . . ." Another hesitation. Were there two *l*'s? I vowed to give no hint. "Doubtful!" She said the word firmly to signal that she was finished.

"Good." My eyes went to the next word. "Pandemonium." Evangeline looked confident. At least this word was spelled the way it sounded.

She took a breath and, as if on cue, pandemonium broke out on Main Street. A rhythmic murmuring had been nagging at the edges of my awareness and now it increased to a chaotic buzz. It was the voices of many men, punctuated by cymbals and deep-throated gongs.

Miss Jensen led the stampede out to the school yard where we all stood and gaped. Evangeline stayed close on my right. Tony Gustafson stepped up on my left.

I remembered the funeral for Tony's grandma. It was all bottled-up weeping and silent suffering. There was slow music from the old piano in the church, played kind of quiet as if she were asleep and we were all afraid to wake her.

The Celestial funeral procession was not like that at all.

They banged gongs and beat on drums and, glory be, they exploded firecrackers fit to terrorize a banshee. When I gave it consideration, it seemed to me that was exactly what they intended.

The Chinese miners must have shut down every one of their diggin's between Bounty and Golden, and China Shacks must have been empty as birds' nests in January. The Celestials were all busy burying China Joe.

First came the musicians, or maybe noisemakers is a better word, for I didn't recognize any tune. I did think the noise would keep away even the most determined demon, and I understood enough by then to realize that was part of its purpose.

Sam Wise followed, holding the King's Umbrella aloft. Mirrors and gold fringe shimmered with his every step. Behind him came clusters of Chinese, each group headed by a man who bore a silk banner on a pole. I recognized the banners from the joss house and figured they signified particular gods, or maybe particular parties in the Celestial world. The banners fluttered like excited birds in the slight breeze, adding to the general excitement.

Oh, it was a ruckus. Gongs and cymbals crashed. Richly embroidered silk shimmered. The men called out to bystanders. It was almost perfect chaos, then . . . *BANG!* . . . the explosions began.

The *pop* and racket of firecrackers went on and on. Pungent smoke swathed the Chinese mourners and rattled us onlookers almost as much as the noise.

I spotted Uncle Shoon. He looked frail, but he walked with dignity in front of a horse-drawn cart. That cart rattled and jolted past the school and up Cemetery Hill, giving a bumpy ride to China Joe's plain wood coffin.

I couldn't bear to look at the coffin itself. The picture it brought to my mind wasn't of the man whose smile was like crinkled paper. The only picture I could conjure was Leeana weeping.

Leeana and her mother followed the coffin with small steps. With their heads deeply bowed and their hands clasped at their waists, they were a picture of sorrow.

Other townsfolk had gathered beside Main Street as sure as they would on the Fourth of July. Mrs. Wilson stood back from the crowd, stiff-backed. It was clear that her pickle heart was set firm against the heathen display.

Some folks followed the funeral up Cemetery Hill. Miss Jensen looked to me as if she yearned to follow, but she sighed and herded us back into the school. We didn't gain much school learning, though. Distant voices hinted at much more interesting goings-on than could be found in books.

Liza had a deep calm that I mistrusted. She looked prim and righteous. "What a shame." She shook her head sorrowfully, but her face was full of satisfaction. "That poor man, to be all alone out there and suffer such an awful accident. He would have been much better off home in China with his own kind."

Tony Gustafson snorted from across the aisle. "A bullet hole is certain-sure no accident! He'd have been better off if he'd been left alone. He wasn't hurting anyone with his grass mining and beekeeping, even if he did make an enemy or two lately. It wasn't any kind of accident. It was murder."

"A Chinee murder doesn't count. Celestials aren't even properly human. It's more of an extermination." The voice behind us was one of the Wilsons. "He'd have been better off if he had gone back to China and let Americans earn a living off of their own land. The other dang Chinee had better pay attention."

His voice dropped to a deeper, quiet tone. "That goes for his white Chinee friends, too."

Liza shushed him and we concentrated on looking as if we were working. I stared at my open book and considered. I was sure the only one in the school who could be called a friend of China Joe was me.

The funeral noise still rolled down the hill when Miss Jensen dismissed school. She herded us through the door and pulled it firmly shut, then set off toward the commotion. Evangeline and I didn't ask permission to tag along. We just fell into step beside her.

The Celestials had gathered on the east-facing slope of Cemetery Hill, where there was a section set out special for them. Miss Jensen explained the location.

"Celestials are particular about how their graves are laid out. The dead person's head must lie to the east, for that is the direction of new beginnings. It helps ensure good luck in the afterlife."

I thought, but didn't say, that as far as I could tell the need for luck was much diminished when a person had already died.

Oh, the noise! I suppose we were part of a funeral service, but the straight-up truth is it was more like a celebration. It didn't sound at all like the dignified worship my family preferred, but I was no longer surprised at that. I had come to expect the Chinese way would be unusual.

We found Leeana and her mother and stood with them. Mrs. Lee managed a little smile for us and put her arm around Evangeline. Leeana said, "Hi," and tried to be polite, but it was hard to know if she was really aware of us standing there.

At last the hubbub subsided and people started to wander back to town. Miss Jensen left us at the school yard.

"I'm truly sorry for your trouble, Mrs. Lee. We like to think we're civilized here in Bounty, but sometimes I wonder if our difficult life doesn't make us more savage than ever."

Mrs. Lee nodded acknowledgment, but she offered no words. We turned to walk through town together in silence.

I had never thought of our life as difficult. The work was hard and never-ending, but I had always felt safe with my family close around me, and I had never really needed anything I couldn't have. I did admit my *wants* sometimes went unrealized, but I thought that was the way in everyone's life. I looked into the distance at the rolling hills and pale mountains. They offered crops and timber for houses. They offered game: deer and elk and salmon. I felt the beginnings of regret that they also offered gold.

When we reached the edge of China Shacks, I hesitated a moment. Mama had said not to go there without an adult, and especially not to take Evangeline. Still, I did not feel that I could desert Leeana once again. I hoped Mama would agree that this occasion was an exception, and there was some comfort in the fact that Mrs. Lee was with us.

My excuses wouldn't have mattered a whit, for Evangeline didn't falter. She kept step with Mrs. Lee right past the livery and along into China Shacks. I had to skip a few paces to catch up.

A noisy crowd had gathered around Uncle Shoon and Sam Wise in front of the joss house. Mrs. Lee nodded to the men there and kept her dignified progress toward home. She greeted the men along the way with quiet dignity but no words, and gradually we made our way to the north edge of town.

Their house looked perfectly normal at first, with a wisp of smoke rising from the chimney and Buttermilk grazing quietly in the side yard. I did notice the iron shutters closed tight over the windows, but I thought that must be part of the mourning, for they had been closed over the windows of Sam Wise's grocery, too.

As we approached the porch, I felt Mrs. Lee stiffen beside me, then she shrieked. Leeana dashed to the door. She turned to face us, hiding something with her body. Mrs. Lee gasped and grabbed her chest. Leeana reached out to support her mother, and I saw it.

Nailed to the door was a long black braid. It could only be China Joe's queue.

Chapter
23

❖

WE HAD LEFT LEEANA and her mother huddled together in their dark kitchen. Mama stood by our door and watched us come from the south, knowing full well we must have come through China Shacks. She had heard the funeral, for the sounds of gongs and firecrackers carried far. Evangeline clung to Mama and told her about the Celestial procession, except she called it a "parade."

Evangeline's voice was lively until she reached the scene at Mrs. Lee's house. She cried when she described China Joe's queue hanging limp on their door.

"Hush, child. I understand Celestial men need their pigtails to keep honor and be welcomed back into their society. He won't have to face dishonor now, because he won't be going back to China."

A voice from the doorway interrupted her.

"Not unless they send his bones back in a jar." Jasper stomped in, with Tom crowding after. Jasper held a newspaper, which he snapped open with a gunshot sound.

"Listen to this." He read the headline extra loud. "Good Riddance to the Celestial Pests."

He read on with increasing satisfaction. "Celestial poachers have been routed from claims along the lower Rogue River. A group of citizens, fed up with the filth and animal squalor bred by the heathens, has launched a movement to return the interlopers to China. Last Saturday night, twenty Chinamen were taken from claims between Blossom Bar and the mouth of the Rogue. They were given enough time to dress and pack a few belongings, then escorted downriver to board the steamship *Fairweather.* Their gold, which was after all taken from American soil, was confiscated and used to buy passage to San Francisco. Once there, Captain Norris was instructed to send the pests back to their homeland.

"We applaud the ingenuity of these citizens. John Chinaman has sojourned in our land far too long. We have nothing in common with these brutish heathens. They exhaust our mineral resources and bring nothing to our land. Rather, through natural cunning and cheating, they steal away with the natural birthright of all Americans. We say 'good riddance.'"

Jasper looked over the paper at Mama to see what effect the news was having. Before she could say anything, Tom spoke. His voice brimmed with excitement.

"It's the perfect solution, Mama. We can use these fellows' own gold to send them back to China."

He glanced at Jasper, and he took on a tone of calm reason that worried me a sight more than excitement. "This way no one has to get hurt, and we can still preserve the gold fields for honest Americans."

"I'm not convinced that no one is getting hurt." Mama spoke extra calm, too. "My girls just witnessed a funeral for a Celestial who clearly did get hurt."

Jasper fairly exploded. He turned to me and shouted.

"I thought you kids were told to stay away from those dang Celestials. You're both fools, and Angelena, you're the biggest dang fool of all. Those devils are worse than animals. In the future, you stay right clear of them!"

I was going to tempt his anger, then, and ask him straight-out why he felt it was necessary to shoot at unarmed men and why he led my brother to those same wicked practices. The words roiled within me and I sucked in breath to holler them. I certain-sure would have thrown them right into the face of Mama's beloved brother, except her voice rose strong between us.

"This was a special time, Jasper. Angelena was doing her Christian duty. If you don't mind too very much, I will tend to my own daughters. You have a mighty difficult task tending to yourself!"

I was amazed. I had never heard Mama speak harshly to Jasper. He seemed amazed, too. He slapped the paper on the table and stomped out the door. Tom, looking bewildered, followed him.

Mama sighed and turned to dinner-making. Her shoulders told me she was discouraged in a way I had never seen before. I set Evangeline to watching Reuben and went to help her.

This was an unusual mood for Mama. When she started to speak in a low voice, I listened.

"Angelena, I am truly sorry about your friend's trouble, but my first concern has to be our own family. There may be more violence. Promise me that you will stay away from China Shacks. And make certain-sure that Evangeline stays away, too."

She rinsed her hands and, pulling a towel from its hook, scrubbed them dry ferociously. "Now, you take Evangeline to feed the chickens while I mix up the biscuits. Your pa will be home soon, and he'll be hungry."

The barn was dry and dim. It smelled of hay and the warm, sweet breath of Molly, our old milk cow. She shifted in her stall when we came in, and Evangeline slipped in to stroke her and croon sweet comforts. I filled a bucket with feed and went to the chicken yard to scatter it among the hens.

When I went into the barn to put the bucket back, Evangeline was still in Molly's stall. She called out to me in a voice of hushed alarm.

"Angelena. Come look at this."

In the back corner of the stall, cushioned in a deep bed of hay, lay an object that was soft green. Wordlessly,

Evangeline picked it up. Gently, she brushed wisps of hay aside.

"It's Kuan Yin. How did she get here? Angelena? How . . ."

Evangeline ran out of words. Bewilderment and horror struggled in her face.

"I don't know." It was the only answer I could speak, for horror had my tongue in bondage, too. The only sensible way to explain China Joe's statue being in Molly's stall was that Tom had brought it. Or Jasper.

"Maybe someone found it." Even Evangeline couldn't speak aloud a possible name of that someone.

"That must be it." I was relieved for the idea. "Maybe some of the fellows went to China Joe's house after news of his death reached town. Maybe it's here for safekeeping."

That last sounded false, even to me. Whatever the true story, there was no good reason for Tom or Jasper to have China Joe's precious statue. It made me sick to think how far Tom might have gone in his foolish regard for Jasper's folly.

"What should we do?" She cradled Kuan Yin and looked very sad.

"Whoever took it, it would shame the family to have it known. We'll give it thought, and maybe talk to Mama. For now, let's just put it back."

She tucked the statue away and we trudged back to the house. Mama was just taking biscuits out of the oven. She was still so grieved about the goings-on in town that I could not bring myself to mention the statue that evening, and Evangeline was content to follow my lead. But though I may not have talked to Mama, I was determined to take the first chance to pin Tom down.

He stayed out late that night, though, and I had to go to bed before he came in. The next morning, he and Pa left early for the diggin's. I went to school as usual, but nothing felt usual anymore.

There was a tenseness in the air that morning, but I figured it must be left over from the funeral doings. At lunchtime, Liza was especially sweet to me and I hoped she was making up for her harsh words the day before.

"I know a secret." Her eyes were bright with it.

"What's it about?"

"Promise you won't tell?"

It seemed to me that everyone wanted promises from me and the whole world was riddled with secrets. Where only a month before I had felt the comfort of familiar friends and places, suddenly nothing was the way it appeared. Liza and Tom had secrets. China Shacks was a forbidden place right inside my own town. China Joe, a gentle man, was dead by violence.

"I won't tell."

She leaned toward me, close as chicks under a hen, and whispered. "China Shacks will burn tonight. By tomorrow morning, all those heathens will be on their way home, one way or another."

"Who said so?" I thought I knew the answer, but I wondered if the Wilson boys really had the nerve to do what they threatened.

"Hush!" She reared up and looked over her shoulder, but no one was near enough to hear us. The little kids were playing tic-tac-toe and the Wilson boys had gone down to the bakery for lunch. Tony Gustafson sat by himself out on the steps, whittling and whistling.

Liza moved close again. "The town's had enough. The murder of that Chinee out at Deer Island just proves they can't be trusted at all. They're starting a Chinee war and next thing you know they'll be after us whites, too. We have to protect ourselves, you know."

"Protect ourselves." I repeated her words dumbly. Who had protected China Joe? Who had protected Uncle Shoon? I wasn't so foolish as to believe he had really fallen off the burro, at least not without encouragement from some "honest American."

It hadn't been another Chinese who had nailed China Joe's queue to Mrs. Lee's door. It would be unthinkable for any Celestial to do that. I had an idea of some non-Celestials who might think of it, though.

I had an idea some of those non-Celestials were in my own family. If violence was so close, actually inside my home, then nowhere was safe, and no one could truly be protected.

"Did the Wilson boys tell you this?" I asked, knowing the answer.

She preened. "They talk to me a lot, you know. They said they're going to show those heathens who's boss and what's right. I reckon they know what they're doing."

I could believe the "who's boss" part. I was considerable less certain than Liza was about "what's right." "Why would they tell you?"

Her eyes looked directly into mine in a way that made me see she wasn't fooling. "Special friends. Loyal and true, like you are, not deceitful and pagan, like some."

So my oldest friend, Liza, thought I was loyal and true. That didn't make me feel at all proud, for how could I be loyal and true to my own kind, and also to my new Celestial friend? The straight-up truth was, I couldn't.

I finished the school day with a heavy heart. Mama set us to chores right off. I entered the barn, half fearing that the statue would be there and half fearing that it would be gone. It was there, nestled in the corner of Molly's stall.

Evangeline scattered the chicken feed, calling out in clucks and chuckles to the hens. While she was busy, I wrapped Kuan Yin in a bit of kitchen toweling and slipped her into my deep apron pocket. I couldn't bring shame on the family by casting public suspicion on Tom or Jasper, but I could return the goddess to her own people. My heart knew that China Joe would be pleased for Mrs. Lee to have her.

I would take Kuan Yin to the Lees. While I was there, I would warn my friends about the plan to burn China Shacks. It would take a little cleverness, though, for I was determined to honor my promise to keep Evangeline out of danger.

I got two buckets and suggested we pick apples and invite Reuben along. He was tickled to be included and trotted to keep up with us. We stretched to pluck ripe Newtown apples and bent to lay them gently in the buckets. Reuben helped once we made him understand the apples were to stay in the bucket, for he opined it was just as much fun to take them out.

When we had half a bucket each, I told Evangeline I must run a fast errand, and she must watch Reuben tight as old shoes. Of course, she wanted to come with me, but she could not leave the baby. I didn't offer to tell my destination, and she didn't ask, but she said, "Please tell Leeana I am sorry."

Bunkum Creek flowed high and fast, but I had too much hurry in me to let that bother. I fairly danced across the slippery log and ran toward China Shacks. Looking up, I saw a clot of smoke rising. It was far too dense and too dark to be coming from Mrs. Lee's cooking fire. I heard distant shouts and the sound of gongs. I clutched the goddess close and whispered, "Please, Kuan Yin, help us all."

Chapter 24

❖

SMOKE BILLOWED from Sam Wise's grocery. Uncle Shoon, with his wobbly gait and white hair, stood out in the crowd gathering there.

"What happened?" I was just in time to join Mrs. Lee and Leeana as they followed Uncle Shoon.

"We don't know. We heard shouting, and came out to find this." Leeana spoke to me in English, but she and her mother kept up a nonstop conversation in Chinese as we pulled foot up the street.

With the sun's face dimmed by clouds, the scene before us was strangely illuminated by gray sky and flickering orange firelight. A swarm of Celestials had formed a fire brigade. One of the laundrymen stood knee-deep in Bunkum Creek, filling buckets and thrusting them into the waiting hands of his partner. The bucket passed from hand to hand to be emptied on the fire. Water hissed like an angry snake when it hit the flames.

Shouts of alarm mixed with the fire's hiss and roar. Gongs sounded from the joss house. Uncle Shoon tried to help Sam Wise rescue merchandise from his store, but the heat drove them back.

Sam shouted something in Chinese. Leeana pulled me back just in time. I guess he kept fireworks in his back room, and the fire reached them all at once. A tremendous *BOOM!* was followed by a string of rapid explosions. The shutters vibrated and I was glad for them because I think they kept the storefront from exploding outward.

At last I realized their purpose. It was not to contain an explosion from within. These shutters, like the ones on Leeana's house, were to keep explosions of street trouble out. The Celestials had learned to protect themselves.

A new ruckus approached, punctuated by the thud of horses' hooves and men hollering. A gang of riders thundered up, with Jasper at the lead. He sat forward in his saddle, holding his riding whip high. The Wilson boys followed, with Gus on his roan and Gunnar, I suppose, on his dappled mare. A cluster of town ruffians filled out the party. My heart shrank when I recognized Tom.

Slashing on either side with his whip, Jasper rode right through the bucket brigade. Men scattered in all directions. Three fell flat into the mud and had to scuttle away on their hands and knees.

"Let it burn!" He wheeled his horse toward Sam

and Uncle Shoon. "We'll burn the rest of this pestilential rats' nest at sunset. You tell these people to pack up and get out, or we will not be responsible for their safety."

I watched in speechless dismay as my uncle rode among the Celestials, taunting and tormenting the frightened men. Tom hung back, but he did not try to stop them. By his presence, he gave support.

Well, I could give support, too. I stood between Leeana and her mother in a space between two shacks, watching the commotion.

Horses' hooves pounded and stirred the wet street into a gluey mess. Running men stuck and stumbled, which caused much merriment among the horsemen. They shouted and dashed after the retreating Celestials.

An old man who had called me "Angel" hobbled out of a shack, bent under the load of a canvas bag. He stumbled and the bag burst open, spilling its contents: a pair of shoes, blue pants, a bundle that looked like rags to me, and a photograph of a woman and a man.

Jasper's horse reared and came down on the scattered treasures, trampling them into the mud. The old man scampered to the road's edge.

Uncle Shoon appeared beside us. "First Angel, you should not be here. It could be very bad, very soon."

"You'll need help," I said. "They won't hurt you with me here. At least let me walk back to your house with you."

171

We wove through the crowd. The heat and noise faded some as we got to Leeana's house. Uncle Shoon fetched Buttermilk. Leeana and I threw clothing and cooking pots into two huge canvas bags. I felt the weight of Kuan Yin in my apron pocket. I left her there, where she would be safest.

The confusion did not seem to reach Mrs. Lee. She carefully wrapped a stack of papers and photographs in a silk cloth. Her actions were deliberate and calm. She put on three sweaters over her blouse, then an oil slicker, and she directed Leeana to do the same. Uncle Shoon came in, similarly dressed.

The nasty smell of burning wood and cloth filled our nostrils. Shouts and gunshots filled our ears. Then we heard the sound I had dreaded: a most vigorous pounding on the door.

We could not spy out of the window, for the shutters were mercifully shut against the mob. From their bellowed orders, though, it was not hard to know who waited there.

"Come out. We got no need to tolerate Chinee trash stinking up our town."

"Come out or we'll burn you out!"

The smell of kerosene engulfed us. They were throwing it against the door. With sparks blowing in the wind, they wouldn't even have to light a match. The house could be in flames any second.

Uncle Shoon opened the door and indicated that I should be the first one to safety.

"Here come the Chinee strumpets!" The voice buzzed with nasty triumph.

I stepped through the door.

The crowd hushed for a second, then I heard my uncle swear a mighty oath. Jasper looked wild, like a stranger, but he shouted at the men with the kerosene to stop.

"Move aside, Angelena. This is grown-up business. You get on home."

"You got a white Chinee in your house, don't you, Jasper?" It was a Wilson—Gunnar, I think. I was getting so I could tell them apart. One was uglier; the other was nastier.

"Shut up, Gunnar. She's just poisoned by these animals. When we get rid of them, she'll be all right."

Uncle Shoon spoke up beside me. "We will go. No need to cause trouble for anyone." He made a gesture to untie Buttermilk's lead, but Jasper's whip hit the railing beside his hand. Buttermilk pulled back. Uncle Shoon stood with his head bowed.

"Let them take their things, Jasper." I didn't have to think about that. It was plain obvious to me.

Gunnar snorted. "Their things! They stole everything they have from white folks!" He grabbed a can of kerosene, but Jasper gestured for him to hold off.

"I reckon we can let you take a burro full of stolen goods, just out of charity."

Uncle Shoon's shoulders sagged. He was a picture of defeat. Mrs. Lee crooned to him and took his arm.

Leeana supported him from the other side and they led him, in halting steps, from the porch.

"Wait!" Kuan Yin was heavy in my pocket. "You forgot this." I held out the statue, still wrapped in cloth.

Mrs. Lee looked puzzled, but turned to me. The cloth slipped back, revealing the figure of Kuan Yin. The goddess almost glowed in light made shimmery by fire and smoke. Mrs. Lee gasped.

Jasper gasped, too. I knew he recognized the statue, but I also knew he didn't dare admit it.

"This belongs to you, now." I took a step toward them.

From the edge of my vision, a blur changed into Gus Wilson astride his roan. Mud spattered Mrs. Lee's face. Gunnar was next. He whirled his horse and shoved her with his boot. She sprawled forward into the mud. Leeana tried to catch her mother and landed in the mud, too.

Someone shouted, "The slant-eyed strumpets are both down, boys. Damn, I wish it wa'nt so muddy!" The Wilson boys laughed.

They struggled to rise, but the milling horses were a terrible danger, and the horses' riders were even worse. Uncle Shoon reached out to them, but someone pushed him onto his knees. I looked from the scorn in the Wilsons' faces to the terror in Leeana's. Jasper, towering over them, raised his whip.

I held Kuan Yin out before me and stepped into Jasper's path.

His horse reared and backed.

"Get out of my way, Angelena. I'm about fed up with your Chinee-loving antics. You scoot along home, now, before you get yourself hurt."

The jade felt warm in my hands. I took a deep breath of smoky air that felt fresher, somehow, than any air I ever tasted. "No, Jasper."

It was strangely quiet. Distant fires crackled, but no one offered any words. A group of Celestials had gathered at a safe distance. I heard a faint murmur that I took to be recognition of China Joe's statue of Kuan Yin.

The Wilson boys and their friends watched Jasper and he stared down at me. I took another deep breath and faced him straight on.

"They haven't done you any harm at all. They're different from us, is all."

Mrs. Lee and Leeana struggled to their feet. It was easy to stay between him and them. Once I got the hang of it, he wasn't really any more scary than that old rattler, or even the bobcat.

"Be careful, little girl. Your house ain't fireproof." Gus Wilson snarled like a half-whipped dog. So, that was it. Plans to deal with the white Chinee were just as harsh as plans for actual Celestials.

"I can't allow it. You leave them alone."

Jasper scowled down at me. His quirt drummed his boot and I thought he was as frustrated as he was angry. His eyes flitted between my face and the statue.

Another horse pushed forward through the mob.

Tom's voice sounded strong and deep as the Chinese gongs. "Shut up, Gus!"

He reigned Majesty up in front of me. It's hard to describe how tall he looked, and how handsome in that flickering light. He had become a familiar stranger. My brother, who had always protected me, tried to protect me once again. Family, faith, and farm . . . I realized that Tom was doing his best to protect us all. I guess, like me, Tom had finally picked a side and he intended to stick to it.

He looked past the statue and gazed at me. "Come with me now."

"I thank you, Tom, but I have to stay here."

Tom studied the Lees. His eyes, so much like Pa's, settled on the statue for a moment, then he looked at Jasper. He sighed mightily. "She's right, Jasper. It's just a pair of old folks and a girl. Let them be."

Jasper glared at Tom, but Tom sat tall and steady. I saw a firmness settle on his jaw, a bit like Mama's when she is feeling determined. Jasper saw it, too.

"Let them load up and go. We just want to be rid of them, anyway."

Tom helped us load Buttermilk and let Uncle Shoon ride on Majesty. When we had done, one of the rowdies spread more kerosene around Leeana's house. Jasper lit a match and threw it on the porch.

We struggled up Main Street through turmoil, and stopped on the bridge across Bunkum Creek. I watched in heartbroken silence as China Shacks burned.

Chapter 25

❖

PA MET US on the road. He had seen smoke from the diggin's and rushed to help, stopping only to collect assistance in the form of the Gustafsons. When he saw the mob with Jasper in the lead, he looked plumb disgusted.

"You go on home with these folks," he told me. "Your mama's plenty worried." He gave my brother a searching look. "Tom, you stay with them."

Tom escorted us home while Pa and the Gustafsons went to help put out the fires. He was gentle with Mrs. Lee and Leeana, but he took special care of Uncle Shoon, settling him in Pa's chair and offering a splinter from the fire to light his pipe.

They talked for a long time, about farming and mining and traveling. Tom allowed that he had never been more than fifty miles from Bounty. Uncle Shoon told him about San Francisco and the sights to be encountered there.

Mama offered them cinnamon rolls and coffee. She

smiled at the look on Uncle Shoon's face and changed the offer to tea. Tom quieted as the tea was poured then cleared his throat and said, "I reckon I've been some kind of fool lately. I thought I was sticking up for what was right, but I guess I wasn't seeing the whole picture. Things sure got out of hand tonight, and I'm sorry for it."

Mama poured more coffee and tea. She was overflowing with "my poor dears" and "there nows." She did start to scold me for being in China Shacks, but Mrs. Lee spoke up and insisted that I had saved their lives. I thought I had not been so heroic as that, but Leeana and Uncle Shoon added so much praise that I felt it would be rude to contradict them. At the end, Mama was beaming at both Tom and me.

The jade statue of Kuan Yin stood with her blessing smile at the center of our table. "She is the color of spring," Mama said.

Mrs. Lee nodded. "She is the color of new beginnings."

We didn't talk about the fire or the mob. I was afraid that when Mama knew how Jasper had been involved, her heart would break. She didn't mention his name, but she did look up sharply at every sound from outside.

It must have been near midnight when the sound of footsteps finally came, announcing Pa. His face was sooty and he reeked of smoke. He cleaned up as best he could beside the fire, then settled into a makeshift bed on the floor beside Tom.

Tom had insisted that Uncle Shoon sleep in his bed.

Mrs. Lee was in the main bedroom with Mama and Reuben. Leeana squeezed in with me and Evangeline.

Papa's snoring, braided with Tom's, kept me from sleep. One blessing came in the night. I heard the soft *pat-pat* of raindrops on our window. The gentle beginning grew into a welcome rush, and I closed my eyes, grateful for the quenching rains. Their lullaby compelled me to sleep.

Perhaps the dragonfish protected the joss house; perhaps it was the simple fact of autumn rain. For whatever reason, it was spared the flames that devoured the Chinese end of Main Street.

First thing in the morning, Mrs. Lee got up and built the fire. She had sweet buns baking for breakfast. She and Mama settled naturally into all the tasks that mothers do, including directing us in our morning chores. I laughed at Leeana, trying to milk Molly. Evangeline demonstrated, but finally gave up and did it herself.

We would not go to school that day, for the whole town was in a flurry over the fire. Pa and Tom set off in the morning with Uncle Shoon, to see what must be done next. They returned by noon with sorrowful news. Three Chinese men had been killed and, except for the joss house, China Shacks was leveled.

I watched my chance and followed Tom out to the barn after lunch. My questions were abrupt, but I didn't feel any need to shilly-shally. "What do you know about the statue?"

"What statue?"

"Don't fool with me, Tom. That statue of Kuan Yin was right here in this barn. Evangeline found it back in Molly's stall. It was hidden in a pile of hay. It must have been taken from China Joe's cabin, maybe by the person who killed him."

My worst suspicions were out in the open. I feared he would hate me for wondering about him, but I needed answers worse than I dreaded them.

He scowled at me. "I didn't leave it anywhere. Jasper had one like it last Saturday night. He won it off a stranger in a poker game."

I believed Tom. I was even willing to accept Jasper's story, although I didn't actually believe it. It didn't matter, one way or the other. We all knew that nothing would happen to a man who killed a Celestial. The straight-up truth was, in some quarters he would be a hero. But in my heart, and I believe the heart of my mother, Jasper had stepped too far beyond decency to ever be truly welcome in our home.

"Angelena?" Tom looked from his feet to the ceiling. "I just want you to know. I think Jasper is right to worry about us losing prosperity, and the Celestials are partway to blame for that. I always thought I could hang around Jasper's shenanigans without being a part of the worst of them. But I was wrong. When I saw you standing up for those folks . . . well, I realized sticking with family means sticking with you."

His main speech ended. He grinned at me and said, "I still think you sometimes act like a dang fool."

It felt just right to walk back to the house with him, even if he didn't show promise of giving over his teasing ways.

That night, after dinner, it was time to think of the future.

"We'll help you rebuild your house," Pa offered.

Mama spoke up about the sore spot in her heart. "I'm afraid my brother was behind a lot of your pain. The least we can do is shelter you until you can rebuild."

Mrs. Lee smiled a soft smile at Mama. "Thank you a thousand times. We cannot stay here now, I think. We will move north. Many of our countrymen are working on the railroads up on the Columbia River. Maybe they will like home-style food."

Uncle Shoon nodded agreement. Leeana did not express an opinion. In her family, like mine, children were not consulted about such decisions.

They spent one more night with us, and on the next morning they loaded Buttermilk. Uncle Shoon tied knots with his two-fingered hand, slick as willow bark. I was embarrassed to think he had ever frightened me. Mama gave them extra food to carry on their trip. Mrs. Lee wrapped Kuan Yin with extra care and tucked her into Buttermilk's deep basket.

I stood beside Leeana and tried to say good-bye. "I'm sorry you can't stay."

She spoke in low tones, and I think her words came from her heart. "You showed me not to fear all white people. Now, I know it is possible for us to live side by side without bringing harm to each other."

"It's possible," I repeated. Possible didn't sound quite so out of reach as it once had.

They set off as the sun climbed over the distant mountain. Uncle Shoon bowed formally to Mama and Pa, then to Tom, who bowed in return. Finally he turned to Evangeline and me.

"Good-bye, Angels. Thank you."

He strode ahead, leading Buttermilk with a firm pace that contradicted his curved back and white hair. Mrs. Lee followed, after bowing a last good-bye.

Leeana did not bow, or even duck her head. She did not use the mincing gait I had seen that first day of school. She walked tall and proud. Her steps devoured the path toward the village and beyond.

She was the girl who faced down bobcats.

The first time I saw her, Leeana wasn't even her name. Miss Jensen changed it, and that was the start of many changes. As I stood with my family and watched her go, I wondered what other changes would come to her, and to me and my family, and to the gold country.

Evangeline and I stood together to watch our friend set out for new lands and new adventures. Evangeline shouted "Good-bye," but I could not shout. I could only whisper.

"Fare you well, An Li."

Afterword

I NEVER SAW An Li again. I like to imagine that she and her family prospered in the railroad-building camps up north.

Riots against the Chinese spread like forest fires that autumn. From Seattle to San Francisco, in villages and cities all up and down the coast, Celestials were burned out and sent packing. It was a dark time.

Some people hinted that Jasper had something to do with China Joe's death, but nothing ever came of that. It wouldn't have mattered anyway, for he was correct. White men were not convicted of murder if the victim was Chinese. It wasn't really considered murder, and some counted it as a public service.

Jasper left the Rogue River valley. We hear from him now and then as he travels through the mining camps, seeking gold and gambling companions. Mama doesn't speak of him.

Eventually, I married, just as Pa said I would. My Johnny came to find gold, found me instead, and settled down to raise a farm and family. Tom and Reuben are farmers, too. Tony followed his dream of raising fruit trees and grapes. His vineyard is the biggest in the valley.

No one was surprised when Evangeline took a job as a reporter for the *Bounty Bugle*. Eventually she bought the paper, and her editorials concerning newcomers to our region are always kind.

Miss Jensen married and moved up to Golden, but by then I had been to the Normal School in San Francisco, and I was ready to take over teaching at our school.

One afternoon, the spring before I married, I was helping a second-grader with her letters at the sand table. I looked out of the schoolhouse window and observed a Celestial headed up Cemetery Hill with a wagon and a shovel. Within a few days, he had dug up the remains of every Celestial buried there. He came back down the hill with his wagon loaded and headed west toward the harbor at Crescent City.

So China Joe eventually did get home.

Author's Note

THE PICTURE of Chinese life in the gold rush days is as accurate as I could make it. The most unlikely part of the story is that Leeana would be in Bounty at all. Of every one hundred Chinese immigrants, ninety-nine were men. Chinese families were rare. War and famine made life in China difficult. When gold was discovered in the American West in the mid 1800s, many thousands of Chinese crossed the ocean hoping to find prosperity. They mined for gold, but they also worked building railroads. They were welcome as long as their labor was needed. But when the gold mines played out and the railroads were finished, some people wanted the Chinese to go back where they came from.

(The Chinese were called Celestials because China was known as the Celestial Empire.)

The joss house in this story actually exists in Weaverville, California. It has been in continuous use since it was built in 1874, and it did survive a fire, possibly because of the guardian dragons on the roof.

Hydraulic mining was practiced at least until 1974 in southern Oregon. The enormous power of water washed hillsides away like a warm knife cutting through butter. Nowadays, such mining practices are not allowed because of damage to the land.

After the riots referred to in this story, Congress passed a law called the Chinese Exclusion Act that kept Chinese laborers from entering the United States. This dramatically slowed Chinese immigration. The act was finally repealed in 1943.